5-MINUTE

MINUTE

MARVEL

SPIDER-MAN™

STORIES

MARVEL

New York
Los Angeles

"The Story of Spider-Man" adapted by Alison Lowenstein. Illustrated by Todd Nauck
and Hi-Fi Design. Based upon the Marvel comic book series *Spider-Man*.

"Beware the Vulture" written by Alison Lowenstein. Illustrated by Scott Jeralds
and Hi-Fi Design. Based upon the Marvel comic book series *Spider-Man*.

"The Sleepless Spider" written by Scott Peterson. Illustrated by Rick Burchett
and Hi-Fi Design. Based upon the Marvel comic book series *Spider-Man*.

"It's Electric" written by Alison Lowenstein. Illustrated by Rick Burchett
and Hi-Fi Design. Based upon the Marvel comic book series *Spider-Man*.

"The Claws of the Black Cat" written by Brendon Halpin. Illustrated by Todd Nauck
and Hi-Fi Design. Based upon the Marvel comic book series *Spider-Man*.

"Spider-Man at the Beach" written by Alison Lowenstein. Illustrated by Lee Garbett
and Hi-Fi Design. Based upon the Marvel comic book series *Spider-Man*.

"The Fantastic. . .Five?!?" written by Bryan Q. Miller. Illustrated by Rick Burchett
and Hi-Fi Design. Based upon the Marvel comic book series *Spider-Man*.

"The Great Race" written by Alison Lowenstein. Illustrated by Todd Nauck
and Hi-Fi Design. Based upon the Marvel comic book series *Spider-Man*.

"The Spectacular Spider-Fan" written by Bryan Q. Miller. Illustrated by Lee Garbett
and Hi-Fi Design. Based upon the Marvel comic book series *Spider-Man*.

"Mysterio Attacks!" written by Michael Siglain. Illustrated by Rick Burchett
and Hi-Fi Design. Based upon the Marvel comic book series *Spider-Man*.

"Nova's on the Job" written by Elizabeth Schaefer. Illustrated by Scott Jeralds
and Hi-Fi Design. Based upon the Marvel comic book series *Spider-Man*.

"Spider-Man and the Avengers" written by Scott Peterson. Illustrated by Timothy Green II
and Hi-Fi Design. Based upon the Marvel comic book series *Spider-Man*.

Printed in the United States of America.
First Edition
10 9 8 7 6 5 4 3 2
G942-9090-6-14063
ISBN 978-1-4231-7786-9

Cover illustrated by Pat Olliffe, Todd Nauck, Craig Rousseau, and Brian Miller
Storybook designed by Jennifer Redding

MARVEL
marvelkids.com
© 2013 Marvel

SUSTAINABLE FORESTRY INITIATIVE   Certified Sourcing
www.sfiprogram.org
SFI-00993
This Label Applies to Text Stock Only

TABLE OF CONTENTS

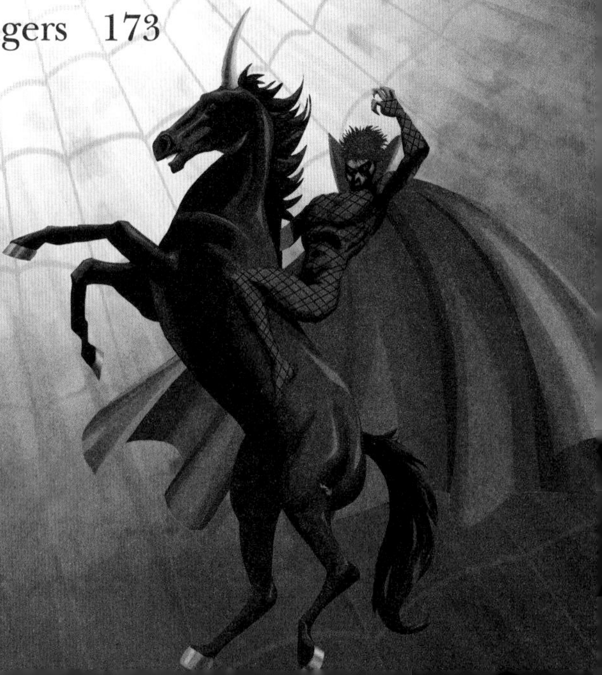

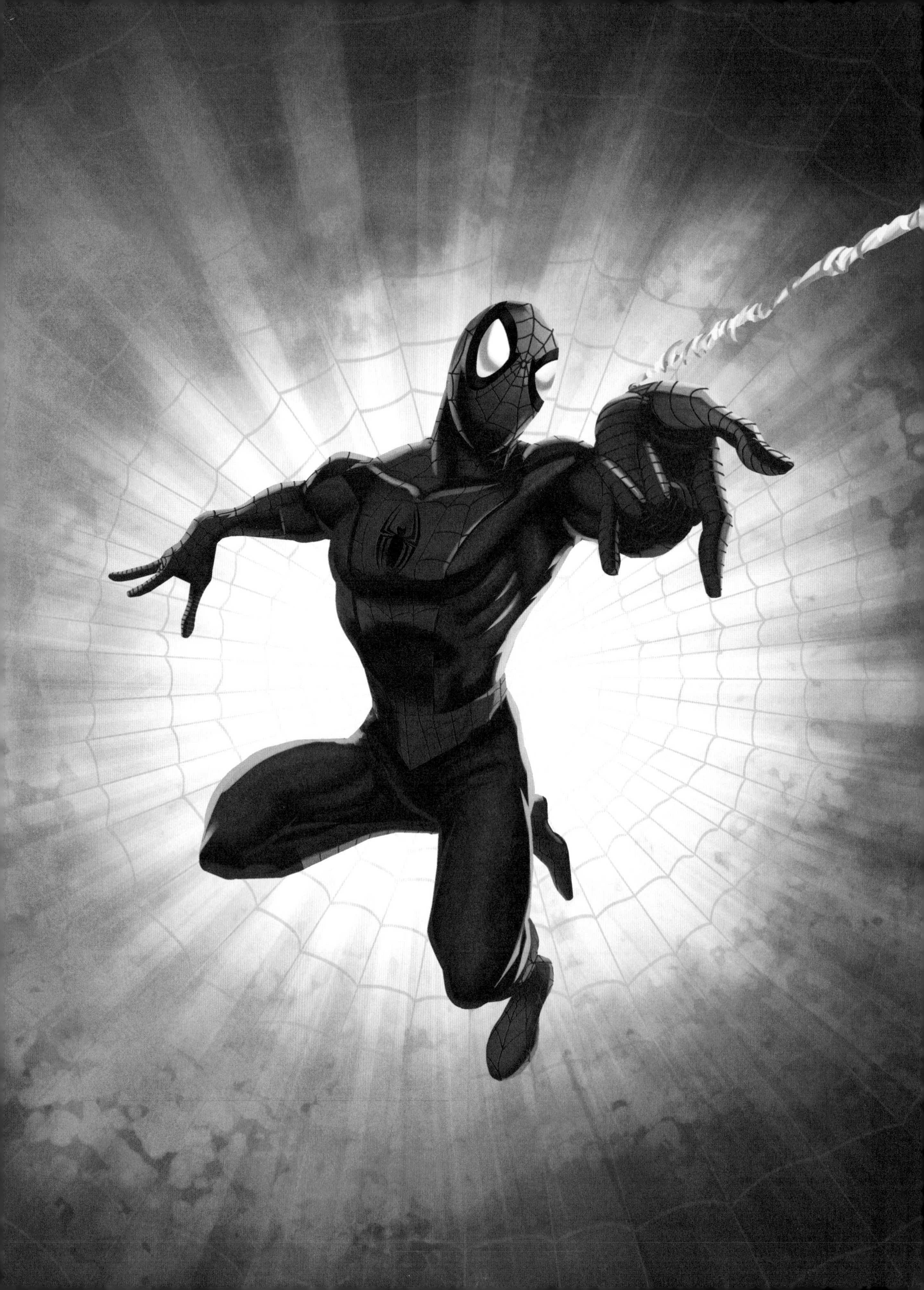

MARVEL
SPIDER-MAN

The Story of Spider-Man

Peter Parker was an average teenager who went to Midtown High School in New York City. He lived in Queens with his aunt May and uncle Ben. Until he was accidently bitten by a radioactive spider, he was just like everybody else. In fact, he had it harder than a lot of other kids did.

Peter was very studious and was one of the smartest kids in his school. But he wasn't very athletic and was often bullied by the kids at Midtown High.

One bully always seemed to find Peter and torment him. This bully was Flash Thompson.

"Hey, you dropped your books," Peter heard Flash say to him as he walked down the hall.

"No, I didn't," Peter replied. Flash pushed him to the ground and Peter's books and papers fell around him.

School might have been tough for Peter, but he was happy at home. He was loved by his aunt May and uncle Ben. Peter's uncle Ben would always tell Peter that he was going to do something special with his life.

"You are so smart, Peter, you can do anything."

"Thanks Uncle Ben. I just want to be a scientist," Peter would say humbly.

"A scientist is a very important job. Peter, science is power. And you should always remember—with great power, comes great responsibility."

"You say that all the time Uncle Ben. How can I forget?"

Then one day Peter's life changed, on a school trip to the Science Hall. Peter was excited to see the scientists at work.

He was so distracted by the exhibits, that he didn't even notice a spider pass through radioactive waves and head toward him.

The radioactive spider bit Peter. He hadn't a clue what an amazing impact this would have on his life. Peter Parker would never be the same.

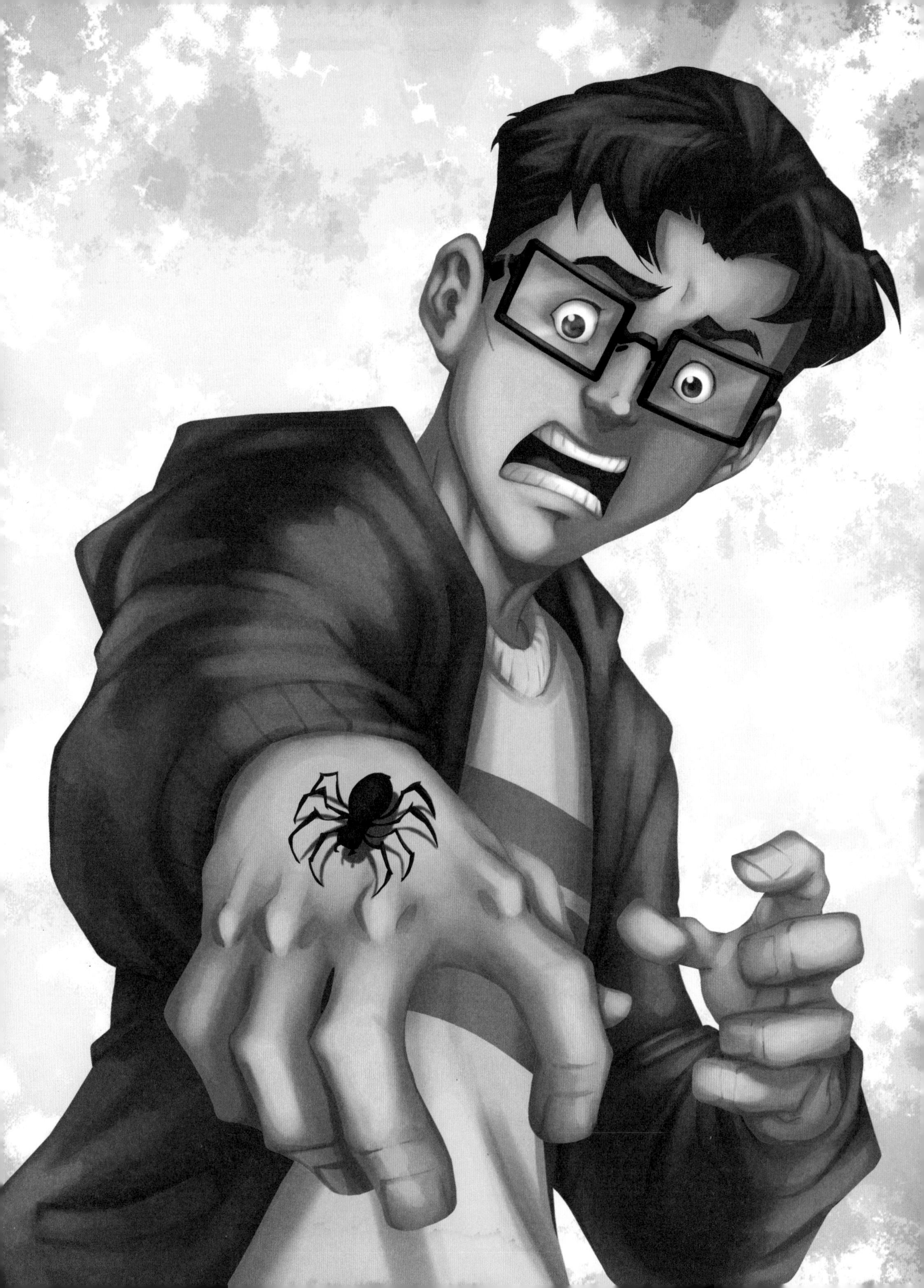

After the bite, Peter adapted many characteristics of a spider. He could cling to walls, he was very strong, and also had "spider-sense." This meant that Peter was able to detect things that were going to happen. These skills made Peter very powerful.

Peter wanted to keep his identity a secret. He created a costume.

Peter worked hard to figure out how to use these new skills. Using his chemistry set, he made webs and tried shooting them in his bedroom.

"This is tougher than I thought," Peter said to himself. "But once I get the hang of this, I will be able to do great things."

Like all teenagers, Peter wanted to make money. He put on his new Spider-Man costume and started to wrestle for cash. Since he had all of these powers, he could beat all of the other wrestlers. One night after a fight, the place where Peter wrestled was being robbed. Since Peter and the owner didn't get along, Peter didn't help the owner catch the criminal.

Later that night, when Peter got home, he found out that a robber had killed Uncle Ben. Aunt May was devastated. So was Peter.

The police officers told Peter not to worry. They had the criminal cornered at an old warehouse. Peter excused himself and went upstairs.

Peter suited up in his Spider-Man costume and swooped over the city. He was determined to avenge his uncle.

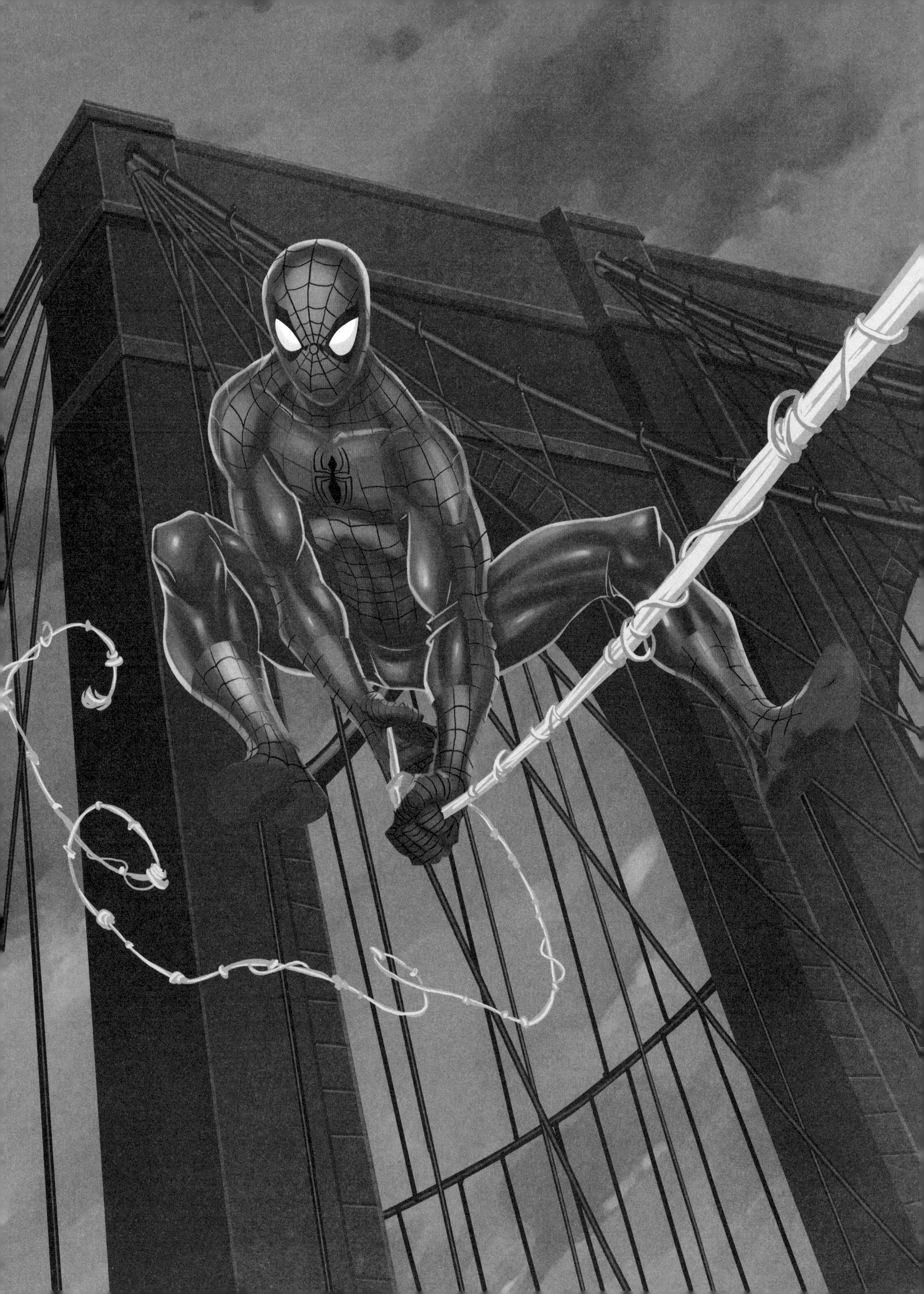

At last, Peter arrived at the warehouse. The thief was stunned. Then Spider-Man sprung into action.

As Spider-Man shot a web and trapped the crook, he got a good look at him—and realized that it was the same criminal he had let escape from the wrestling match!

If only he had stopped him then! If only he had not acted so selfishly!

Peter vowed to help others. He would never let anything like this happen again!

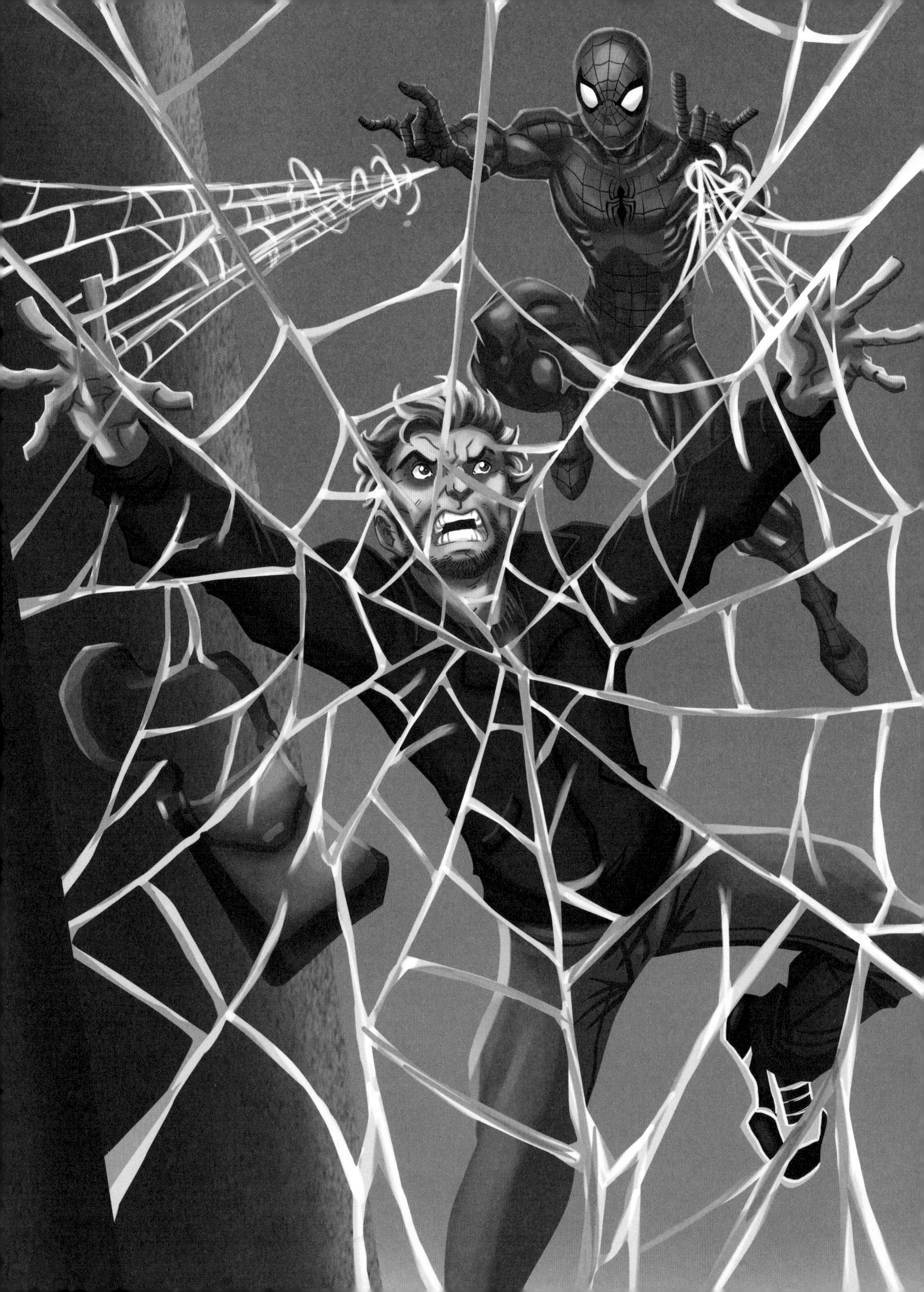

Just a month ago, he would have been busy studying in his bedroom at Aunt May and Uncle Ben's house, but not now. Peter remembered the words that his uncle Ben always used to say: "With great power comes great responsibility." Uncle Ben was his role model.

The next day, the kids at school started to talk about Spider-Man, and Peter listened to them in the halls.

"I think he's okay," Flash said as he looked at an article about Spider-Man. "He's just trying to help the city."

If only Flash knew that Peter was Spider-Man!

That night, Spider-Man heard about a criminal on the loose in Manhattan. He swung across the bridge into the streets to fight the villain, who was trying to rob a store.

Spider-Man felt confident, because he had worked very hard at perfecting his abilities. He caught the criminal.

Sure, Spidey was getting lots of attention. For Peter, it wasn't about money or fame or any rewards his power could give him. Peter wanted to help others.

Peter Parker might seem like your normal teenager, but there is a part of him that makes him extremely special. He is a Super Hero and can scale buildings and spin webs. He is the amazing Spider-Man!

Beware the Vulture

Peter Parker and Gwen Stacy were eating sandwiches and enjoying the sunny day on the Great Lawn in Central Park.

"Isn't this so relaxing, Peter?" Gwen asked and then pointed at the blue sky dotted with clouds. "You couldn't ask for a more perfect day." And she was right—until Peter's spider-sense started to tell him that trouble was brewing.

Peter looked up to see the Vulture soaring over Central Park.

Peter threw over his water bottle in an attempt to distract Gwen. He was also looking for an excuse to get away and change into Spider-Man.

"Gwen," Peter coughed, "I need more water." And off he went to save the day.

Meanwhile, at Stark Tower, billionaire inventor Tony Stark had just come back from testing his new Iron Man armor.

"How was the ride?" his assistant Pepper Potts asked.

"Excellent," Tony replied. "It's fast and powerful. It took a lot of work, but I'm glad I did it. Of course, I'm already thinking of ways to improve it."

"We need to make sure it's secure," Pepper told him. "You never know who might try to steal it."

But before she could finish her thought, they saw the Vulture fly by the large glass window.

"You are always one step ahead, Pepper," Tony said, looking out the window. "Looks like we have a visitor."

Just then, the alarm started to sound throughout Stark Tower.

"We need to protect the armor! If the Vulture gets his hands on it, he'll be as powerful as Iron Man!" Pepper shouted.

"I've got it under control," Tony reassured her, as he rushed off. But when he entered the lab, the Vulture was already there.

"You outdid yourself, Tony," said the villainous Vulture. "I can't wait to fly through the skies in this. Everyone will think *I'm* Iron Man."

"Never!" Tony yelled as the Vulture flew toward him, ready to attack.

Without his armor, Tony was just a regular guy, and fighting the Vulture was next to impossible. The Vulture was wearing his electromagnetic suit, which gave him super-strength and allowed him to fly.

But just as the Vulture was about to attack, a voice called out from behind them.

"Back off, Vulture!" Spider-Man yelled as he swung toward the Vulture and delivered a mighty kick to the chest.

"Nice work, Spidey," Tony called out as he ran toward his Iron Man armor to suit up.

Spider-Man battled the Vulture, but it was time for the Armored Avenger to join the fight!

The Vulture quickly got to his feet. He crashed through
the window in an attempt to escape, but Spider-Man was too fast
for him.

Spidey ran up the side of the building and fired a web right
at the Vulture. It was a direct hit!

The Vulture flew away at top speed, lifting Spider-Man high into the air. Then a red and gold blur rocketed into the sky above them. It was the invincible Iron Man!

"I've got it from here, Spidey," Iron Man said as he fired a repulsor blast at the Vulture.

"Thanks, I.M.," Spidey said as he shot a web at a nearby spire and swung out of the way of the blast.

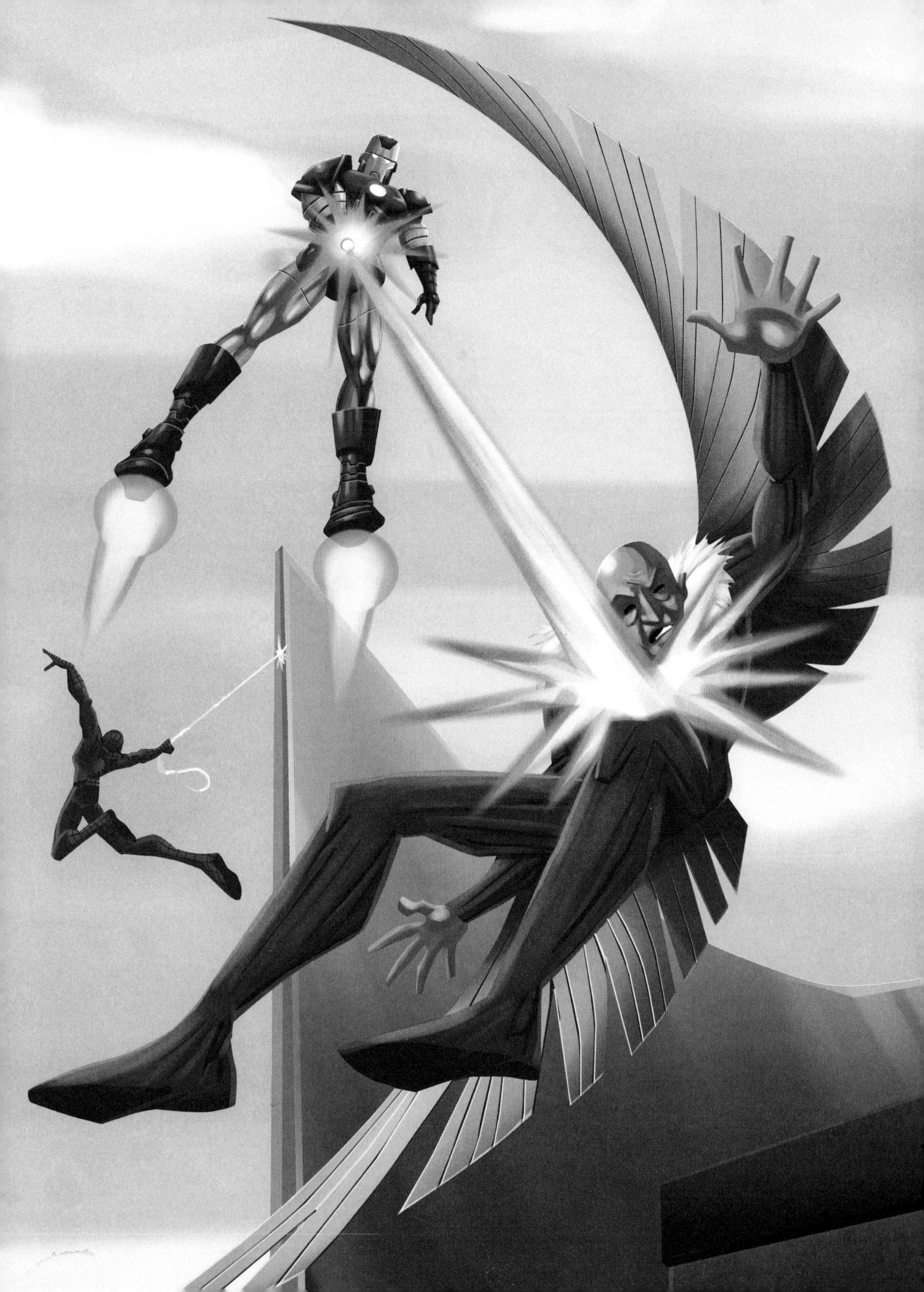

On the roof, Spider-Man and Iron Man teamed up to battle the criminal. Spidey shot webs as Iron Man blasted repulsor beams.

The blasts weakened the Vulture as he tried to fly away from the duo.

"Getting tired?" Spidey asked.

"Never," the Vulture replied.

"Time to clip your wings, Vulture," Spidey said as he fired more and more webs at the villain. "You should know that crime doesn't pay!"

Iron Man landed on the rooftop just as Spider-Man finished webbing up the Vulture.

"You've not seen the last of me!" the Vulture shouted. "I'll break free and then you'll both pay for this!"

"You're not going anywhere, Vulture—except to jail!" Iron Man said.

Later, after the police had taken the Vulture away, Iron Man fired his rocket boosters and blasted off into the sky. "Thanks for the assist, Spidey," Iron Man said to the wall-crawler. "I've got to get back to Stark Tower to fix the security system."

"And I've got to get back to Central Park!" Spidey said to himself after Iron Man flew away. "Gwen must be wondering what happened!"

"You're back!" Gwen said, excited to see Peter. "What took you so long?"

"It took me forever to find a working water fountain," Peter told Gwen, leaving out the part where he turned into Spider-Man and teamed up with Iron Man to defeat the Vulture.

"The sun is so strong, Peter. Bet you're glad you got some water," Gwen said. "It's one of those days where you just want to sit and relax."

"I couldn't agree more," Peter said with a smile.

The Sleepless Spider

Spider-Man has been called a great many things: Amazing; Spectacular; Sensational. But today, no matter how hard Peter Parker tried, he was none of those. Today. . .Spider-Man was very, *very* sleepy.

For the last week, Peter couldn't sleep through the night. His dreams were troubling, silly. . .and sometimes downright spooky. And a week of nightmares makes for one sleepy crime-fighter.

Peter didn't think much of it, however, until one very long spider-yawn almost allowed Shocker to ruin the Policeman's Ball.

Spider-Man groggily swung into action. He webbed Shocker's gauntlets before knocking the vibrating villain to the floor with a well-timed kick.

"Look! Not only is he a menace, but Spider-Man was sleeping on the job!" J. Jonah Jameson shouted from his table as Spider-Man swung away.

Spidey knew he needed to see a specialist, someone who was truly an expert on dreams and the human mind. And he knew just the doctor to call. . . .

"Doctor Strange," Peter began, "I'm sorry to interrupt, but
I've been having trouble..."

". . .SLEEPING!" Doctor Strange said as Spider-Man entered. Stephen Strange knew why Peter had visited him on that dark and stormy night. Strange had felt Peter's troubles long before Spider-Man had come to his doorstep. Doctor Strange threw his arms wide as he conjured the magical Eye of Agamotto. "The eye of Agamotto shows me that you've been having nightmares," Strange told Peter. "And now it will show me those nightmares."

Soon, Doctor Strange was able to see Spider-Man's dreams. In some, he was back in elementary school and forgot to wear his pants. In others he had nightmares about the Sinister Six winning every battle.

Doctor Strange could not only see the future and the past—he was able to see right into a man's very soul. And tonight, he intended to venture inside of Peter Parker's mind!

Strange told Peter, "Your sleep is interrupted not by the natural but by the supernatural, your dreams invaded by the most dastardly of nocturnal threats—your mind is plagued by the villainous Nightmare himself!"

With a snap of his fingers, Strange placed Peter into a deep trance. With the help of the Eye, Strange took a deep breath, then dove into Peter's dreams.

Peter once again found himself pantsless in front of his entire class. And though he was embarrassed, he was no longer alone. Doctor Strange stood tall beside him, urging him to see the nightmare for what it truly was.

"The dream is yours to control," Strange told Peter.

Peter concentrated, and the class vanished. They were replaced by the master of bad dreams, Nightmare, and his trusty steed, Dreamstalker!

"The Sorcerer Supreme commands you to release your hold on this hero!" Strange shouted. But Nightmare simply laughed.

"I take power from dreams, Strange," Nightmare began, "and with a hero as strong as Spider-Man, I'll finally be great enough to defeat you!"

As Strange and Nightmare launched into magical combat
with each other, Peter knew he had to help the Sorcerer
Supreme. In a trance or not, Spider-Man had to lend a hand!

And he realized he knew just how to do it—by using the power
of his mind. By using his imagination!

Peter thought and thought and thought, as hard
as he could. To his amazement, the dream around him
began to change!

They weren't in Peter's school anymore, but on a giant
chessboard, and Spider-Man was in control of the pieces!

"It would seem Spider-Man is using the powers of his own
dreams against you!" Strange declared to Nightmare.

Spidey played move after move, defeating Nightmare's pieces, until the villain was the only one left in play. Outnumbered, the villain retreated, leaving Peter's mind.

"You've won today, Strange, but you've not seen the last of me!" Nightmare shouted as he rode Dreamstalker out of Peter's mind and back to his home in the shadow realm.

"I look forward to defeating you again." Strange smiled.

Peter woke with a start, pleased to find the good Doctor waiting with a warm cup of tea.

Spidey swung home, changed into his pajamas, and slipped under the sheets. There were no monsters under the bed, and the only thing in his closet were his regular clothes and his spider-suits.

So, for the first time in what felt like weeks, Peter Parker finally got a good night's sleep.

MARVEL SPIDER-MAN

It's Electric

It was movie night at Aunt May's house. As Peter, Mary Jane, and Aunt May watched a film, the lights started to flicker and the TV shut off.

"Do you think that it's the fuse box?" Aunt May asked as she and MJ shared a bowl of popcorn.

Peter's spider-sense was telling him that it wasn't the fuse box. So he told them he'd check and headed to the basement, but he was really suiting up and getting ready to find the culprit behind this blackout.

Jessica Drew was visiting New York City with her friend Lindsay. As they walked across the Brooklyn Bridge, they took pictures of the skyline at dusk.

"Hey, it looks like the lights are out in the city," Lindsay said as Jessica took pictures.

Jessica, who was secretly Spider-Woman, had a feeling there was trouble brewing. When she saw Spider-Man swing through Manhattan, she knew she had to help. People on the bridge were pointing at Spider-Man, and Jessica was able to quietly suit up and join the fellow Super Hero without her friend Lindsay noticing.

"Keep the lights on," Spider-Man demanded as he spotted Electro attempting to destroy a utility pole.

"What, are you afraid of the dark?" Electro taunted as he unleashed a bolt of electricity at the wall-crawler.

Electro wanted to rob the gold vault at the Federal Reserve Bank. He was annoyed that Spider-Man was trying to save the day.

"Need some help?" Spider-Woman asked Spider-Man, as she used her super-human power to casually toss a large mail truck at Electro.

Spider-Man smiled. "Nice to see you're in town."

"This was supposed to be a vacation," she joked.

"A Spider-Man and a Spider-Woman. What a treat. I get to fry you both," Electro said.

"Doubtful, Electro. You had better watch your cholesterol. You're the one who is going to end up fried," Spidey told him.

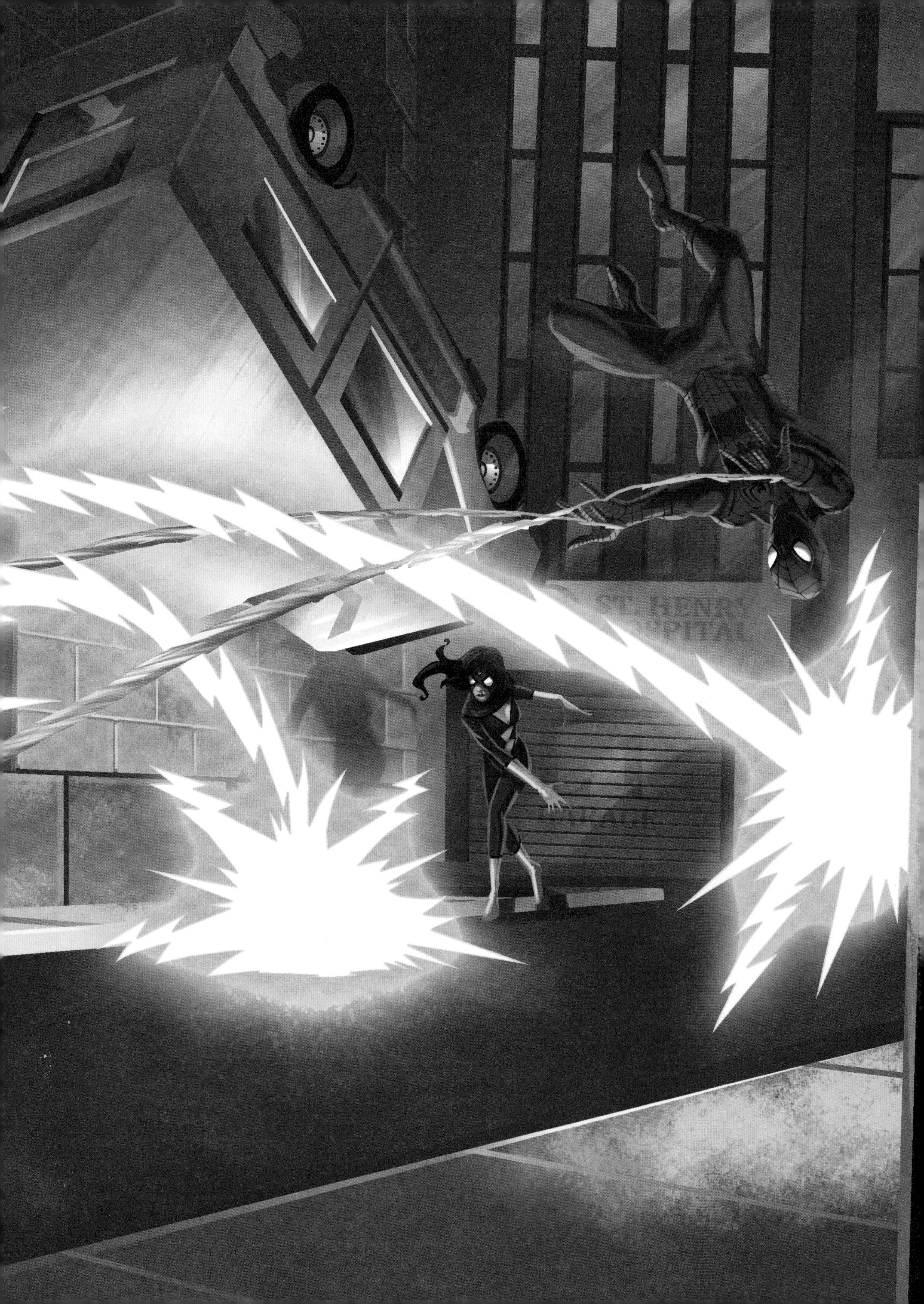

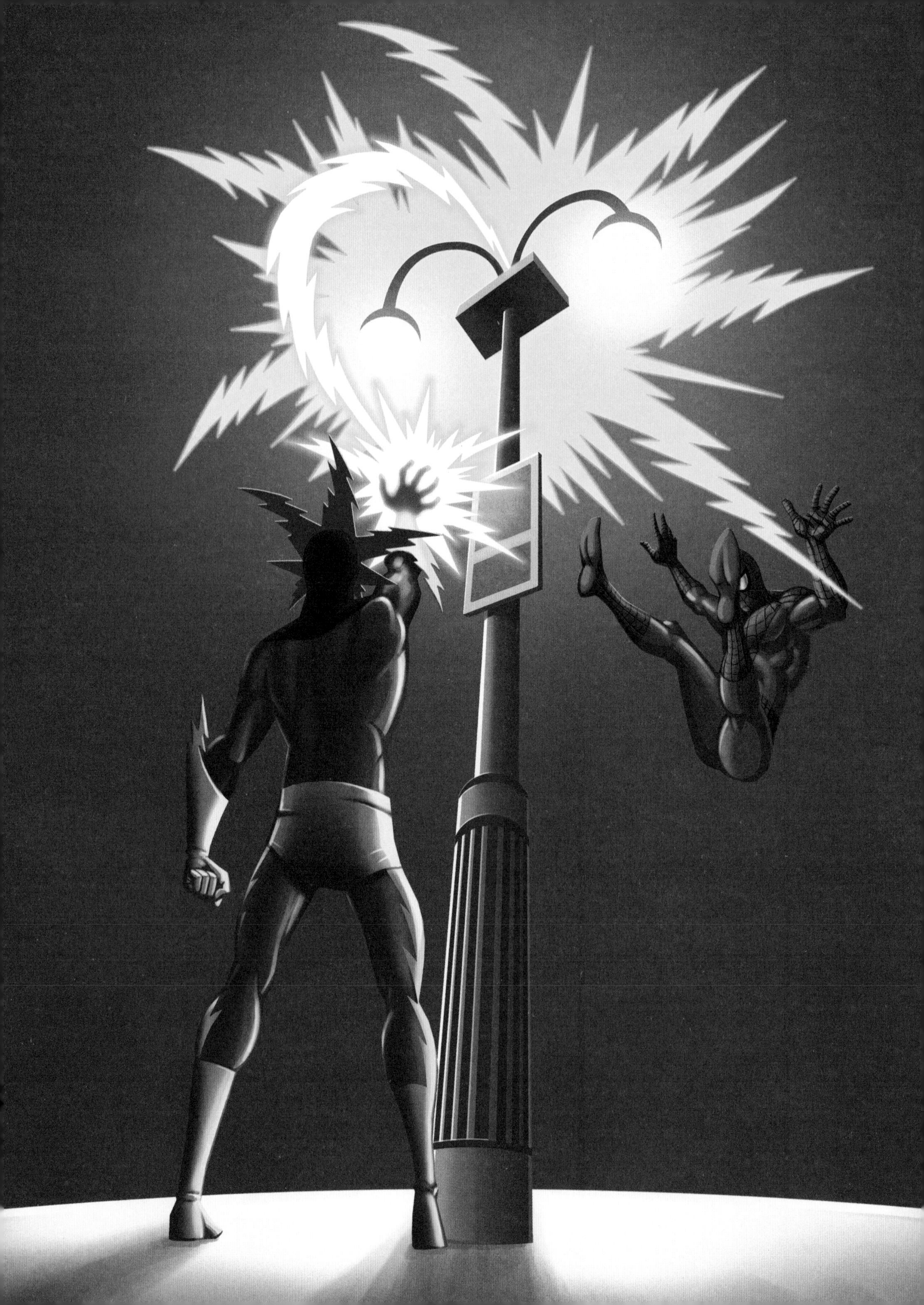

Electro tried to escape from this powerful duo, and fired a massive bolt of electricity at a streetlight, causing it to short. The explosion knocked Spider-Man back!

Spider-Woman confronted Electro, but the Super Villain unleashed another powerful blast. Spider-Woman tried to block it, but was shocked, and Electro escaped.

Electro managed to blast open the door to the reserve and headed straight for the gold vault. But Spider-Man and Spider-Woman were hot on his trail.

Electro fired a massive electric burst, temporarily blinding the heroes, and he ran to the vault where the gold was kept.

Electro turned the large gold wheel, opening
the door to the vault.

"Game over, Electro." Spidey shot a web at Electro,
attaching him to the wheel.

But Electro freed himself and
blasted the door open, saying, "It's
not over until I have my gold."

Spider-Woman knocked Electro onto the gold bricks, and
Spider-Man webbed him down fast. "Now that the power is back
up, every alarm in the city is going off. The police will be here in
minutes," Spider-Woman told him.

"Thanks for the team-up, Spider-Woman," Spidey said.

"I'm so glad I was able to help. Now, I'm off to see the sights!"
Spider-Woman replied as she hurried off to meet her friend.

"You missed some light show," Lindsay said to Jessica as she pointed toward Manhattan. "You could have had some nice photos."

"I'm just glad to get some photos of the New York City skyline at night. It's so beautiful," Jessica said as she snapped some pictures.

Lindsay looked at the map. "Maybe tomorrow we should check out the Federal Reserve. I hear they offer a free tour."

"I've been there before, so let's go someplace else," Jessica said with a smile.

"Sorry it took so long," Peter said as the lights came back on at Aunt May's house.

"You did a great job fixing the fuse box, Peter," Aunt May said with a smile.

"You're my Super Hero," MJ said.

The Claws of the Black Cat

Late one night, two criminals, Boris and Bruno, were about to rob a bank. As Boris planted explosives, Bruno stood guard. They were surprised when a dark figure raced through the alleyway and landed by them.

"Oh, no!" Bruno called out. "We have to run. It's Spider-Man!"

But the figure in the alley wasn't Spider-Man. It was the Black Cat, a master thief.

"The police are on their way," the Black Cat said. "Do you want to stay here and go to jail, or do you want to work for me?"

This wasn't a hard decision. They went with the Black Cat.

The next morning Peter Parker was at work at *The Daily Bugle* and his boss, J. Jonah Jameson, was very upset.

"Parker!" JJJ yelled, "Spider-Man helped two bank robbers escape from the police last night. I want pictures!"

"Spider-Man wouldn't do something like that. I think there must be an error," Peter replied. He knew Spider-Man was innocent because Peter was Spider-Man, and he had been home last night.

"I don't pay you to think. I pay you to take pictures," JJJ barked.

Peter suited up as Spider-Man and searched for the real criminal who had helped the bank robbers escape. As he perched on an American flag from a rooftop, he saw a masked woman dressed in black swing into a nearby warehouse. He followed her. He knew it! It was the Black Cat. Spider-Man had to act fast!

Spider-Man shot webs at the Black Cat, but she dodged them. The Black Cat hid in the shadows, safe from Spider-Man's webs.

Like a cat, she seemed to have nine lives and always wound up on her feet. She was also very fast.

Spidey lost her. He didn't notice her sneaky escape through a broken window.

Back at her hideout, the Black Cat told Bruno and Boris her new plan.

"Boys, we have to break into jail."

"Break *into* jail?" Bruno was shocked. "That's crazy!"

"There's nothing to worry about; we won't be staying very long. I just need to get an old friend of mine. His name is Gadget, and he can build us all the tools we need to rob every bank in the city! The plans for the jail are in this box. Study them, so we can be prepared!" the Black Cat told the criminals.

They weren't pleased. Hearing the word *jail* made them shudder. They certainly didn't want to be a part of this plan, but there was no way out.

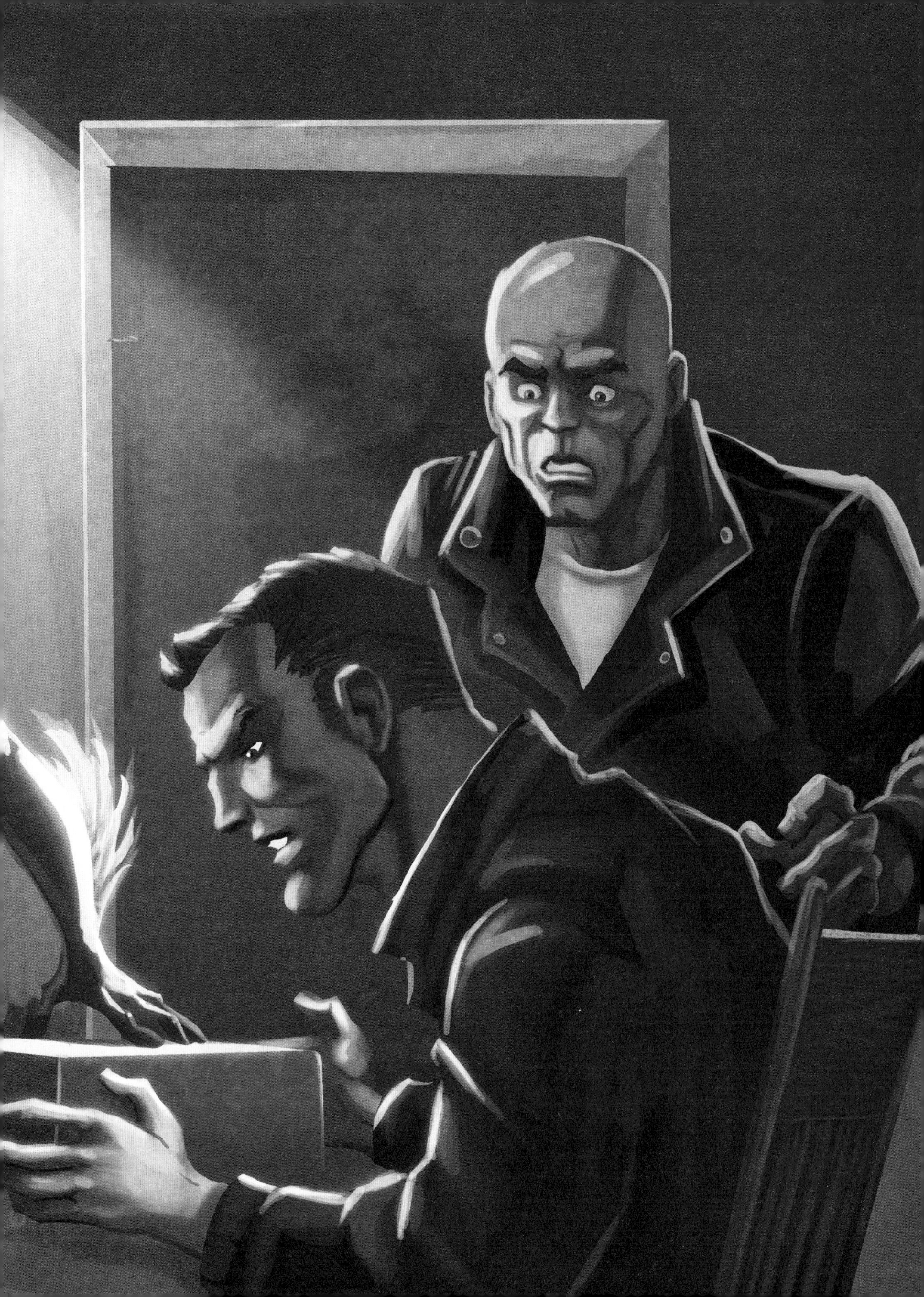

Peter Parker had set up a camera when he was chasing the Black Cat. He walked into *The Daily Bugle* with the pictures he had taken. Peter showed them to Jameson.

Peter said, "Spider-Man's chasing the Black Cat. She must have been the one who rescued those bank robbers from the police."

"They probably work together!" Jameson told Peter. "This is just two criminals trying to figure out how to split the loot."

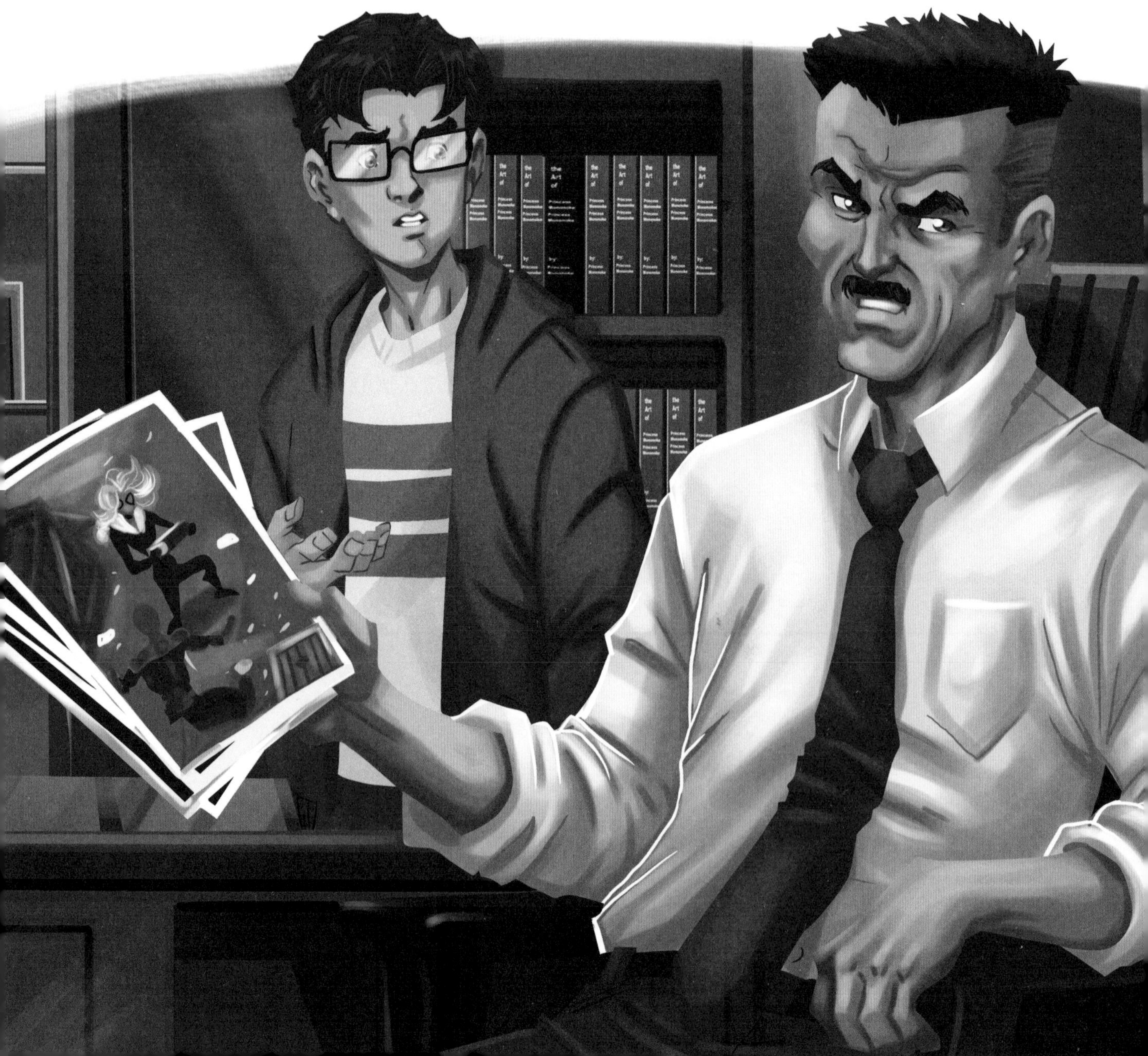

A television in the newsroom of *The Daily Bugle* gave Peter the answers he was looking for. "We repeat: There's been a break-in at police headquarters," the newscaster said. "Nothing was stolen except the plans for East River Prison."

Spidey swung into action, and he arrived at the prison just
as the Black Cat was lowering herself down the wall of the prison
on a rope.

"Here, kitty, kitty!" Spidey called.

The Black Cat spun around. "Back for more?" she asked. "You're
in trouble, young man. Now, Boris!"

Just then, Boris triggered the explosives he had put in place. The wall of the prison fell apart, and Spidey fell right along with it.

Several officers pulled the rubble off of Spider-Man. They thanked him for trying to prevent the jailbreak, but Spider-Man was embarrassed. The Black Cat had gotten away. However, Spidey already had a plan.

Spidey spoke to the guards and learned Gadget's real address. Then, he went to Gadget's house. Gadget was really a retired engineer named Miles Stitchson.

When Spider-Man arrived, he found Boris and Bruno and fired his web-shooters.

"Hey, why don't you guys hang around until the police get here?" Spidey said as he wrapped them up in webbing.

Just then the Black Cat opened the door. She was shocked to find Spider-Man waving back at her.

"It's time for you to give up," Spidey said to the Black Cat.

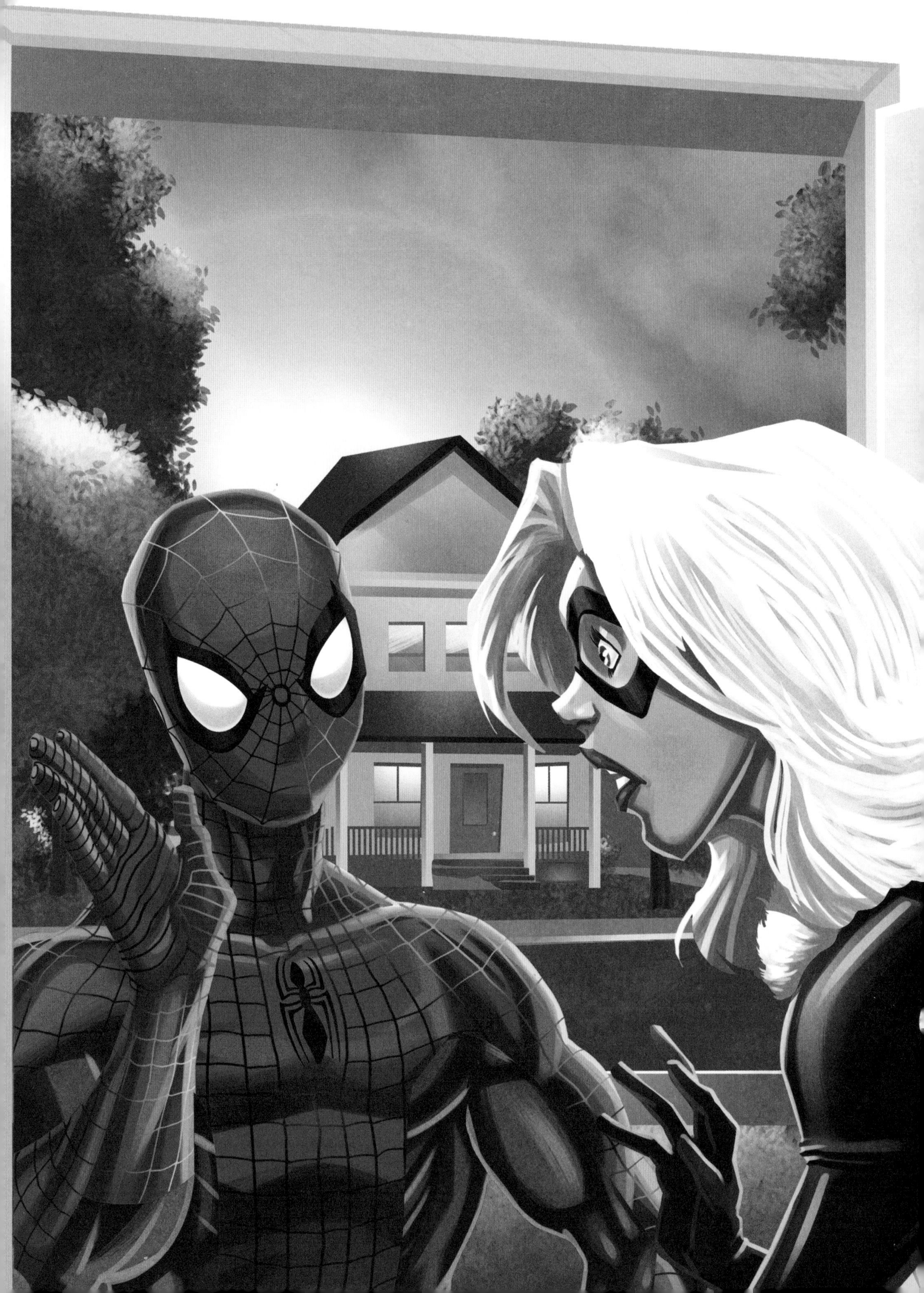

"Never!" the Black Cat cried. She leaped right at Spider-Man, but he ducked out of the way and she went flying over him. With incredible speed, she swung from the doorway, and landed on the roof of the house.

"Stick around!" Spidey said as the Black Cat stuck to the roof of the house. He had covered it in sticky webbing.

When the police arrived, they were very happy to take Boris and Bruno into custody. But the Black Cat had gotten away again! She'd left her boots stuck to the roof and escaped.

"That cat really does have nine lives," Spider-Man said. "I have a feeling we'll meet again."

"Thanks for capturing Bruno and Boris and leading us back to Gadget," one of the police officers said to Spider-Man.

The next morning, Peter Parker walked into the offices of *The Daily Bugle*. "Well," he said to J. Jonah Jameson, "it looks like Spider-Man is a hero after all. He captured the bank robbers and the escaped prisoner."

"But he let the Black Cat get away! That wall-crawler may have everyone else fooled, but not me!" JJJ yelled. "And who wrote this headline, anyway?"

Peter picked up a copy of *The Daily Bugle* and smiled. It read SPIDER-MAN: HERO!

Spider-Man at the Beach

Mary Jane Watson let out a scream as she rode the Cyclone at Coney Island.

"Have you ever been on anything so terrifying?" MJ asked as they exited the ride and walked toward the ice cream shop.

"Nope, that was scary all right. It really goes fast for an old roller coaster," Peter replied with a smile. If only Mary Jane knew Peter was Spider-Man, and the night before he had climbed up a skyscraper and caught a villain. Then she'd know that he wasn't really scared on the ride.

CYCLONE

Peter and MJ licked their ice cream cones and headed to the beach. As they made their way off the boardwalk and toward the water, Peter's spider-sense started to tingle. People ran past them screaming. Beachgoers grabbed their towels and bags.

Peter stopped a boy carrying a bag of beach toys and asked, "What's going on?"

"They are trying to take over the beach," the boy replied.

Peter looked out and saw someone in the sand. It was Sandman, and he wasn't making a sand castle—he was making trouble.

"I need to throw out this ice cream cone," Peter told MJ and snuck off, quickly returning as Spider-Man. The crowd on the boardwalk stopped in awe as Spidey raced toward the sandy beach.

"You might be made of sand, but this isn't your place in the sun," Spider-Man said as he shot a web at Sandman.

"A web isn't strong enough to hold me," Sandman said as he swung a fist at Spidey.

Spider-Man pushed Sandman. As Sandman fell back, Spidey was confident this would be an easy fight, until he heard a familiar laugh behind him.

Doctor Octopus grabbed at Spider-Man with one of his tentacles.

"I thought I smelled something fishy," Spider-Man said, pushing Doc Ock's tentacles away.

"It's over, Spider-Man. The city is mine." Doc Ock tried to grab Spider-Man again but Spidey jumped to avoid the tentacles.

Sandman got up, throwing a punch at Spider-Man, but Spidey avoided it. Battling two villains wasn't easy. The sun was strong and beating down on the beach, and Spider-Man was hot and thirsty. He wished he still had his ice cream cone as he dodged tentacles and a menace made of sand.

Just then, Doc Ock's tentacles grabbed hold of Spidey and he couldn't break lose. Spider-Man was in trouble! Doc Ock smiled. "Now you are captured. There's no web that you can spin that will get you out of this, Spider-Man."

Then Sandman got in on the action. Sandman punched Spider-Man with all of his might, knocking Spidey out of the tentacles and onto the sand.

"Look what you did!" Doc Ock yelled at Sandman. "You set him free."

"You two make a great team," Spider-Man joked as he leaped up.

Sandman raced toward the boardwalk. The crowd of onlookers fled in terror.

"Run as fast as you can!" Sandman screamed to the crowd.

He headed toward the amusement park on the boardwalk. Spidey knew he was up to no good. He wanted to chase Sandman, but he was still trying to stop Doc Ock. Battling two criminals was a juggle, but he knew he had to do it.

Spider-Man turned to Doc Ock. "Give up, Doc. It looks like your sandy partner in crime is now dust in the wind. He's *desert*-ed you."

"Deserted. Very funny. You were always one with a pun."

"I aim to please." Spidey smiled as he fired a web at Doc Ock's face.

"I never needed Sandman. I have my own plan, which he never knew about. I'm going to create a huge wave that will flood the city! Then I will take charge!" Doc Ock confessed with a loud maniacal laugh!

The waves were getting higher and Spider-Man was worried they would start to flood the beach. He shot as many webs as he could in an attempt to stop Doc Ock.

Spider-Man tried to reason with Doc Ock. "Stop the wind, Ock. The water might be home to a real octopus, but you'll never be able to escape the waves."

Doc Ock realized that Spider-Man might be right, but he wasn't about to give up now!

Spider-Man shot his webs and wove them around all four of Doc Ock's tentacles as the villain fell to the ground with a thud, trapped and helpless.

"Gotcha. You're not going to slip out of this grip," Spidey said as he fired more webs. Doc Ock couldn't move.

"This isn't going to work," Doc Ock said, trying to use his tentacles to break free.

"Looks like it has. You're stuck in the sun. Bet you wish you packed some sunscreen," Spidey joked.

Meanwhile Sandman was grabbing all of the cash from the ticket booths at the amusement park as people ran away in fear. Sandman grew more excited as the bag of loot got heavier. He was going to be rich, and Spider-Man was too distracted with Doc Ock to fight him. His plan was working.

As Sandman grabbed money from the last booth, Spider-Man jumped down from the Ferris wheel and leaped at him.

"Buying a ticket to the fun house?" Spidey asked as he knocked Sandman down. Sandman's bag of cash fell open and the money started to blow away in the wind.

"Looks like you're blowing your money," Spider-Man said as he shot a web at Sandman.

Cornered, Sandman looked around for Doc Ock.

"If you're looking for the doctor, he is caught up in a web," said Spidey. Then the web-slinger fired even more webs at Sandman. "Seems like you might have had different plans, but you both wound up in the same place."

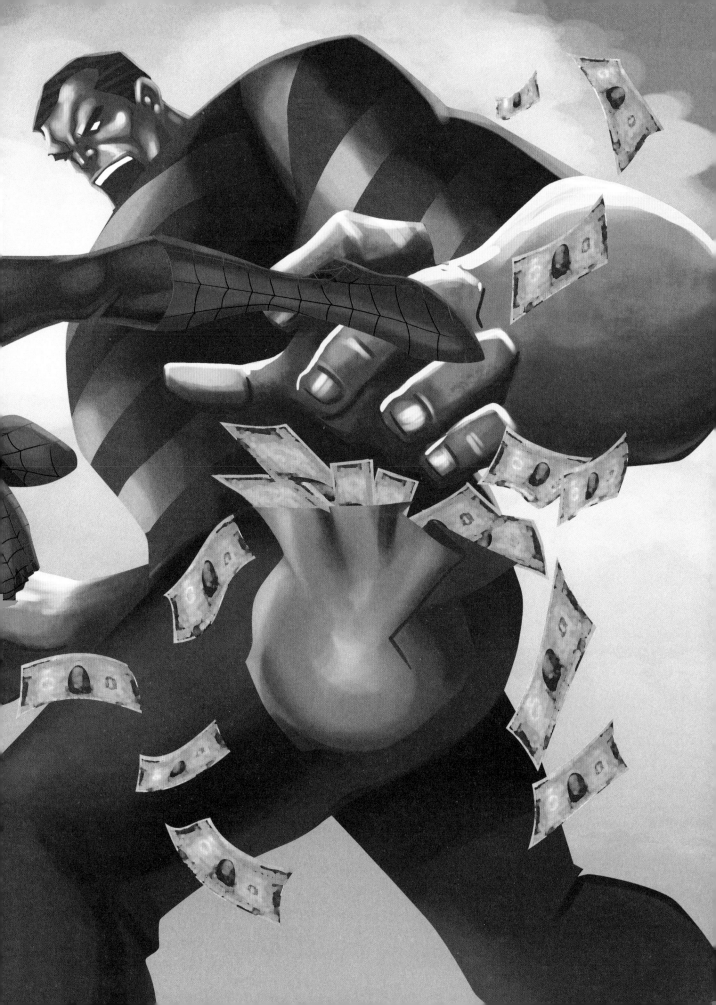

Spidey attached a webbed Sandman to the Ferris wheel.
"It's your lucky day, Sandy. You get a free ride. Too bad your
friend is stuck on the beach," Spidey said. Then he remembered
Mary Jane. He had to find her in the crowd.

As the beachgoers made their way back to the boardwalk,
they cheered for Spider-Man. As he swung over the crowd,
Spidey wasn't thinking about all of the attention; he was too
concerned with finding MJ.

After searching the crowd, he saw her in front of the
ice cream shop.

"Peter, where were you?" MJ asked.

"I went to throw out my cone, and then I saw all the commotion and came looking for you."

"I was in the ice cream shop," MJ replied. "Thankfully, you're safe. Were you able to see Spider-Man?"

"I just saw him for a second. I wanted to stay out of trouble." Peter smirked.

"Want to go on some rides?" MJ asked.

"Sure—just not the Ferris wheel," Peter said with a grin.

The Fantastic. . .Five?!?

As often happened on Mondays (but *never* Wednesdays) Peter Parker found himself fighting hand-to-hand-to-hand-to-hand. . . with the nefarious Doctor Octopus!

"Seriously, Otto, how long does it take you to clean up for dinner?" he joked as he dodged attack after attack.

"Long enough to learn how to truly get the drop on you," Doc Ock cackled.

Peter evaded one tentacle, but was slammed with another. And this was no ordinary tentacle; Doctor Octopus had attached a sinister syringe to the end.

In a flash, Otto injected Spider-Man with a mysterious silver liquid! Suddenly, Peter's vision blurred and his head started to spin. Peter needed to see a doctor, and not the kind with mechanical limbs! Spider-Man realized he was losing his grip. . . .

Lucky for Spidey, the Fantastic Four had just thwarted one of Mole Man's many invasion attempts (which *also* happened on Mondays), and were speeding through the air below.

Doc Ock quickly made his escape as the FF flew close to catch a falling Spider-Man.

"Need a lift?" Ben "The Thing" Grimm asked as he caught Spider-Man.

"Reed, he looks ill," the Invisible Woman told her husband.

"You're right, Sue," Mr. Fantastic told his wife. "We'd better get him back to my lab."

Peter woke, strapped to a medical table. He was groggy, sore, and powerless, but relieved to see that he was in good hands.

"Am I gonna make it, Doc?" Peter asked Mr. Fantastic and the rest of the Fantastic Four.

"Octavius didn't inject you with a virus or a bacteria," Reed began. "We found tiny Nanoctobots in your bloodstream."

"We think he's trying to shut down your spider powers," Sue added.

"Otto's always gotten under my skin, but this is ridiculous!" Spidey coughed.

"H.E.R.B.I.E.," Reed called out to the FF's robot assistant. "Activate the Fantasti-ray!"

"This will make us shrink down, so we can go inside your blood and battle the Nanoctobots," Reed explained to Peter. And in a flash of light, the FF were gone!

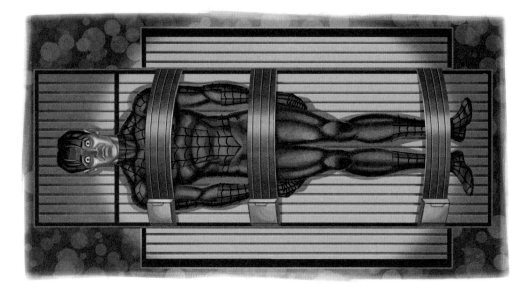

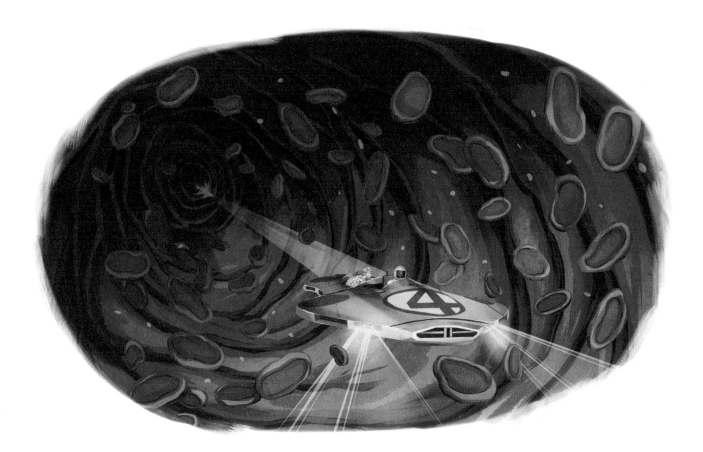

Aboard the Fantasticar, the FF explored the almost alien world, dodging blood cells and zapping germs until they found the dangerous Nanoctobots. They were harming Peter from the inside out!

"Time to flame on!" Johnny said, ready for action.

"No! Not here!" Mr. Fantastic yelled. He couldn't chance Johnny turning into the Human Torch inside Peter's blood. He quickly stretched his arm and grabbed Johnny before he could flame on.

"We're going to have to do this the old-fashioned way, with our wits and our fists," Reed said.

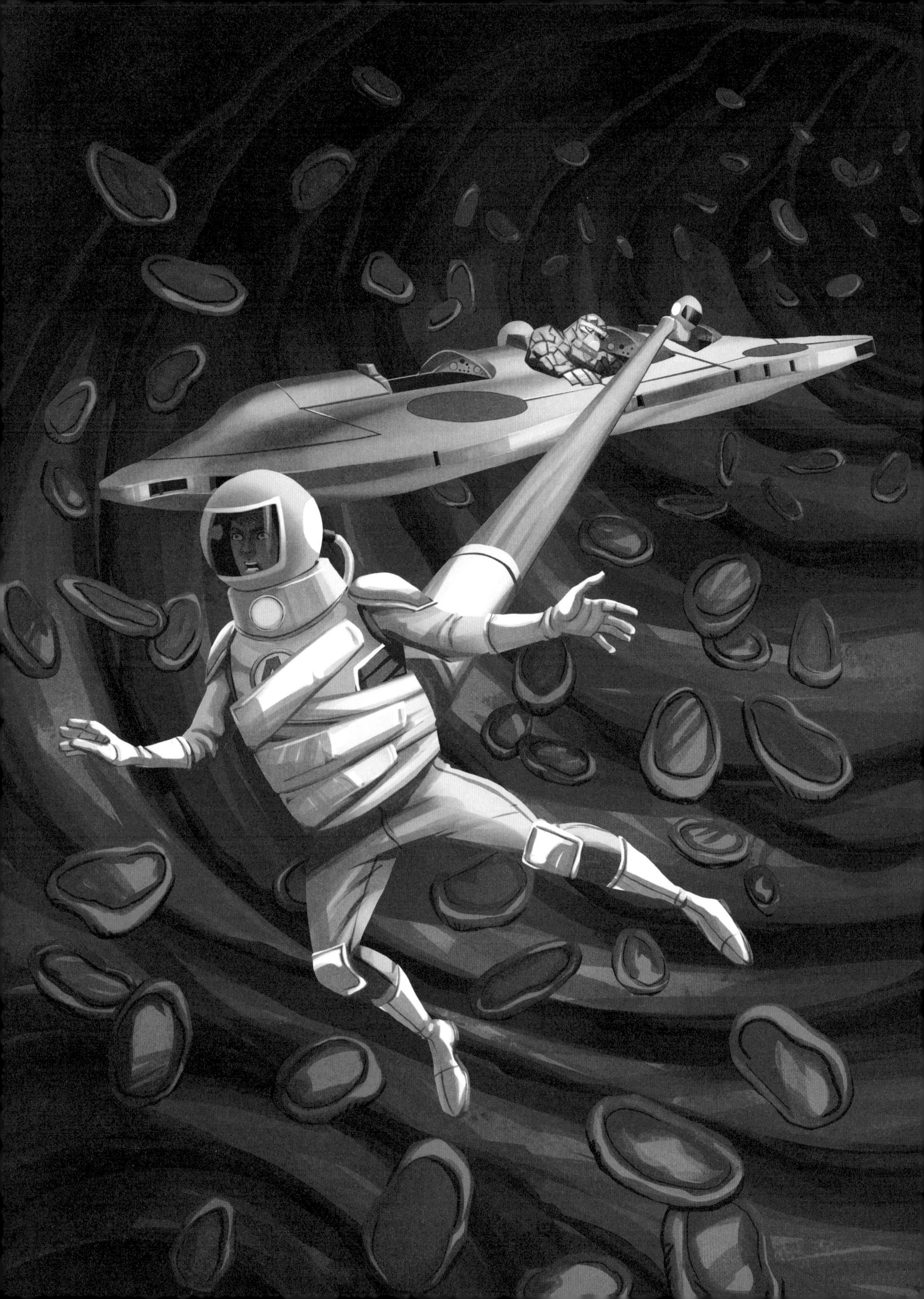

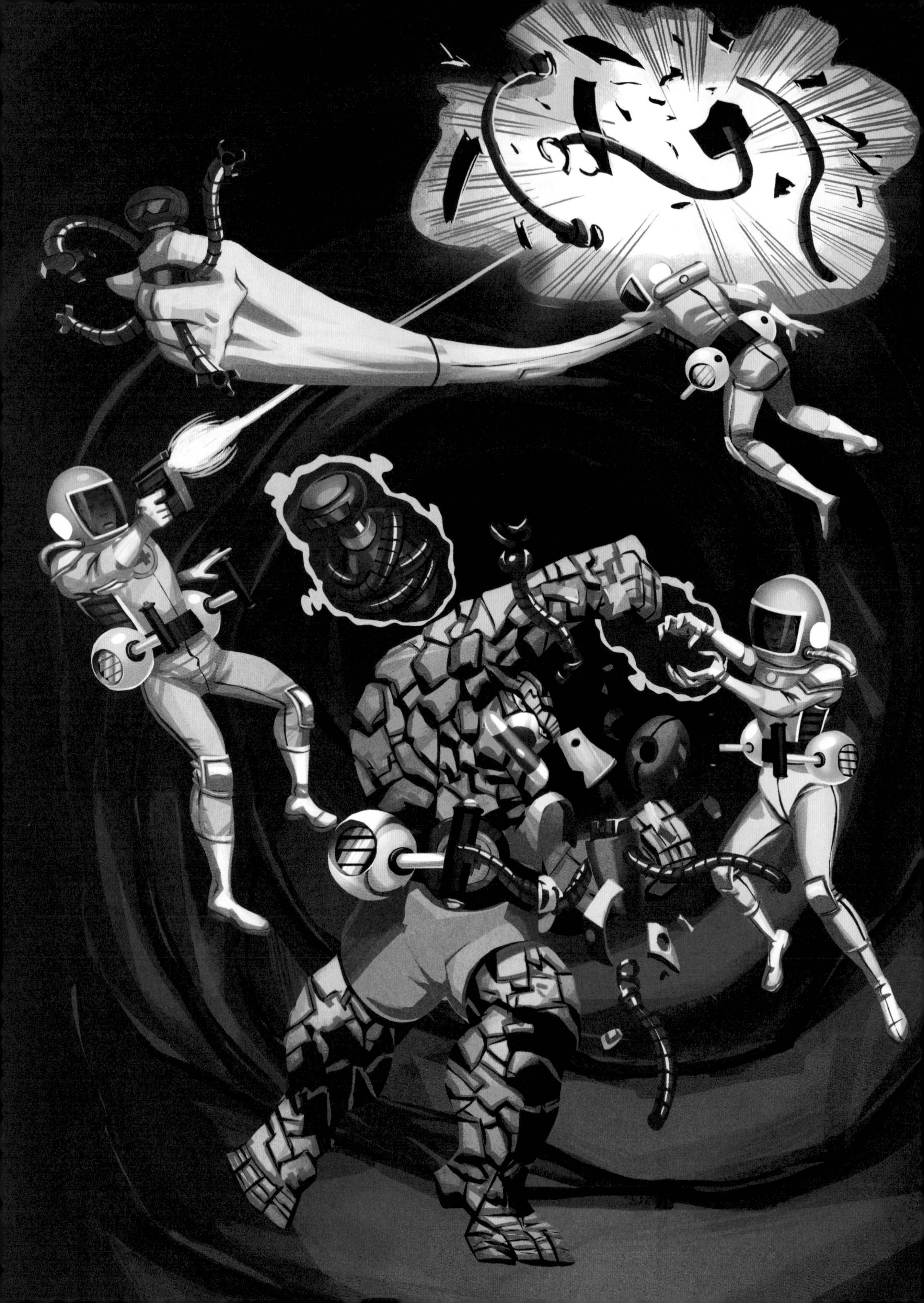

"Then it's clobberin' time!" Thing shouted as the Fantastic Four launched into battle.

Back in the lab, alarms sounded as Doc Ock breached the Baxter Building's defenses and burst into the lab!

"I had hoped my machines would send you to your doom," Doctor Octopus growled. "But without the Fantastic Four to protect you, I'll get to finish you off myself!"

"They're closer than you think," Spidey replied as he stumbled away from Octavius. Spidey needed his powers back, and fast!

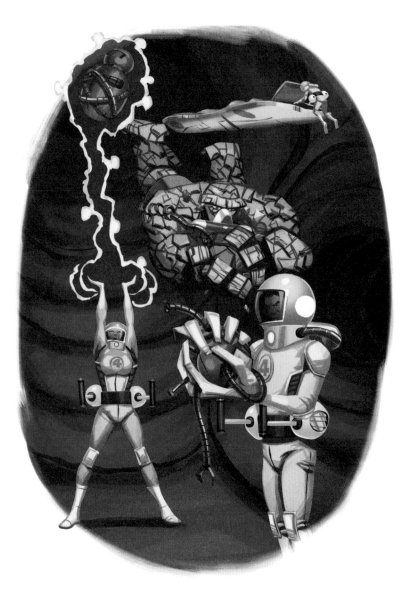

Meanwhile Sue Storm trapped the last robot inside one of her force bubbles, then crushed it to pieces. She and the team then gathered the rest of the wreckage—the last thing Peter needed was tiny robot parts sloshing around in his veins for the rest of his life!

Suddenly, the world around them shook.

"H.E.R.B.I.E.," Reed shouted into his communicator, "activate the Fantasti-ray and get us out of here! Spider-Man's in trouble!"

"You got that right," Spider-Man's voice responded over the radio. "But H.E.R.B.I.E. is a little tied up right now!"

"How do you feel, Spider-Man?" Doc Ock asked, ready to crush the hero.

But with the Nanoctobots now defeated, Peter's powers slowly began to return. He couldn't help but smile under his mask.

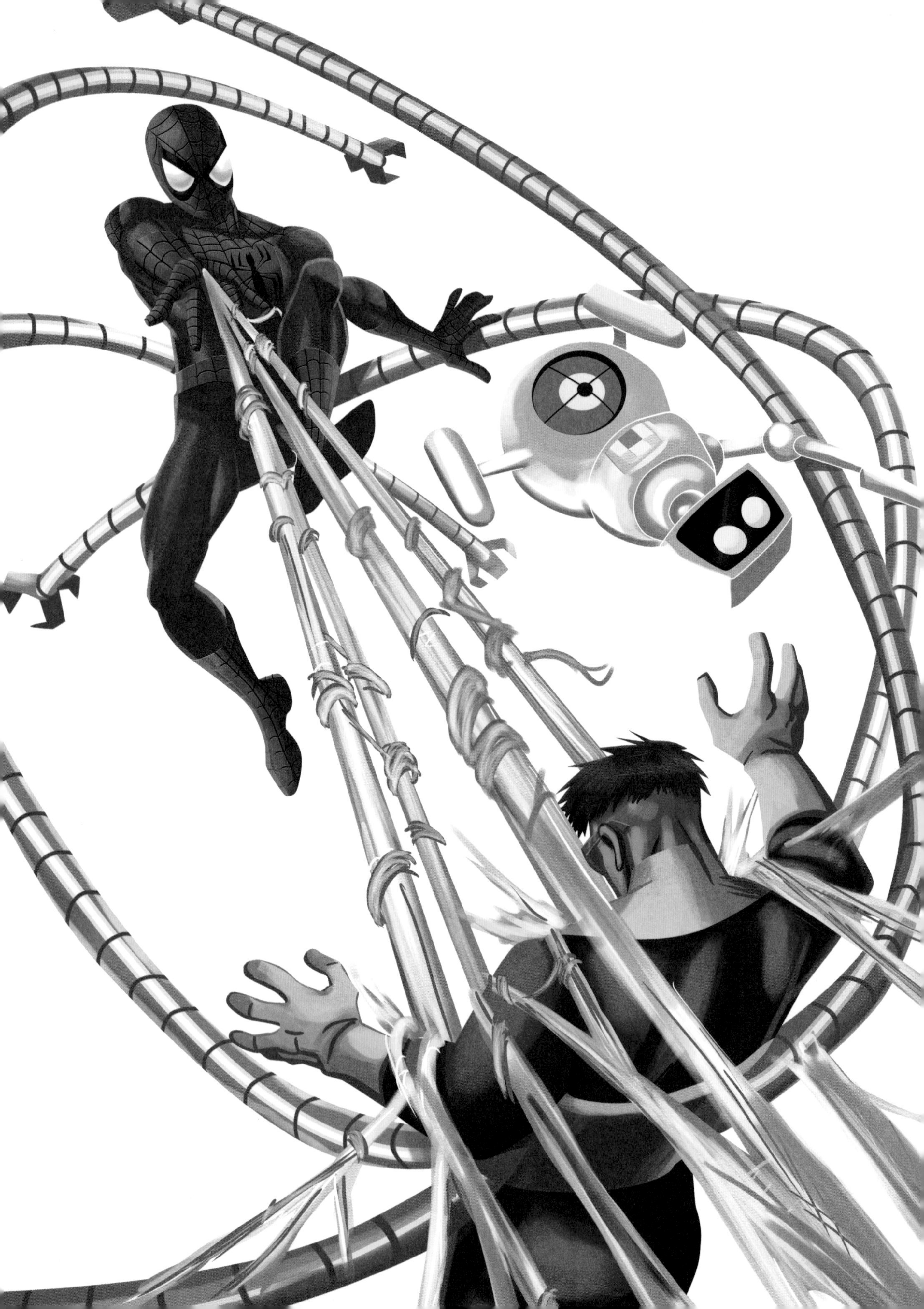

Spider-Man sprung into action and webbed Doc Ock to the wall, then vaulted for the Fantasti-ray controls.

"I feel *amazing*!" Spidey exclaimed.

With a blinding flash of light, the Fantastic Four were transported from within Peter's body and returned to their normal size!

"Can I 'flame-on' now?" an excited Johnny asked.

"Be my guest," said Spider-Man with a smile. "Those webs won't hold Doc Ock for long!"

United, Spider-Man and the Fantastic Four easily defeated
the evil Doctor Octopus.

Later that morning, the Fantastic Four treated Peter to breakfast.

Peter toasted the heroes. "Thanks for everything! I feel great!"

Suddenly, Johnny crinkled his nose, shut his eyelids tight. . .
and let loose a tremendous sneeze!

"I think I might be coming down with something, and I swear it
isn't a case of Nanoctobots!" Johnny wheezed.

"No. . .but it just might be the common cold," Reed considered.

"Anyone up for another fantastic voyage?" Sue asked.

"Except maybe now," Peter cut in, "Spider-Man gets to shrink down to size. To the Fantasti-ray!"

The Great Race

Peter Parker knew Dr. Curtis Connors was in trouble. With a picture of the Lizard splashed across the cover of *The Daily Bugle*, Peter Parker could only imagine what sort of trouble Connors was in.

Peter also knew that his boss, J. Jonah Jameson, would be mad that he didn't have exclusive snapshots of the Lizard. Jameson relied on Peter for these types of photos.

When Peter walked into *The Daily Bugle*, J. Jonah Jameson called him into his office.

"Parker, the Lizard is on the loose and I need pictures," JJJ demanded. "I don't care if you have to camp out in a swamp. I want a shot for the front page. And I also want a picture of Spider-Man fighting the Lizard," JJJ said with a grin. He thought he was asking the impossible, but he expected perfection.

"I'm your man. I'll get you shots," Peter told his boss.

Meanwhile, Dr. Connors's wife was very upset. She had seen her husband mixing up a strange formula earlier that week. She knew that he was trying to create a serum that would help him grow his missing arm back, but she also knew that it came with a serious side effect. It turned Dr. Connors into an evil villain called the Lizard.

Spider-Man found Mrs. Connors sitting on her porch. She was staring at a picture of her husband.

"I wish he didn't care about growing that arm back." She looked at Spidey with concern.

"I'll find him," Spidey told Mrs. Connors. "Don't worry."

"You need to bring him to the lab and feed him the antidote."

"Got it! He won't be a lawless lizard for much longer. Soon he will be back to being good old Dr. Connors."

Spidey searched all through New York City and finally spotted the Lizard. Spider-Man chased him into an ice cream shop, hoping to lock the cold-blooded beast in a freezer, which would diminish the Lizard's strength, but the Lizard escaped, crashing through the window.

"I'm not a fan of frozen treats," the Lizard called out to Spidey.

"If you try to run from me, you're going to be on a Rocky Road," Spidey taunted.

The Lizard stomped through the streets, creating a wave of destruction, crushing car windows and damaging storefronts.

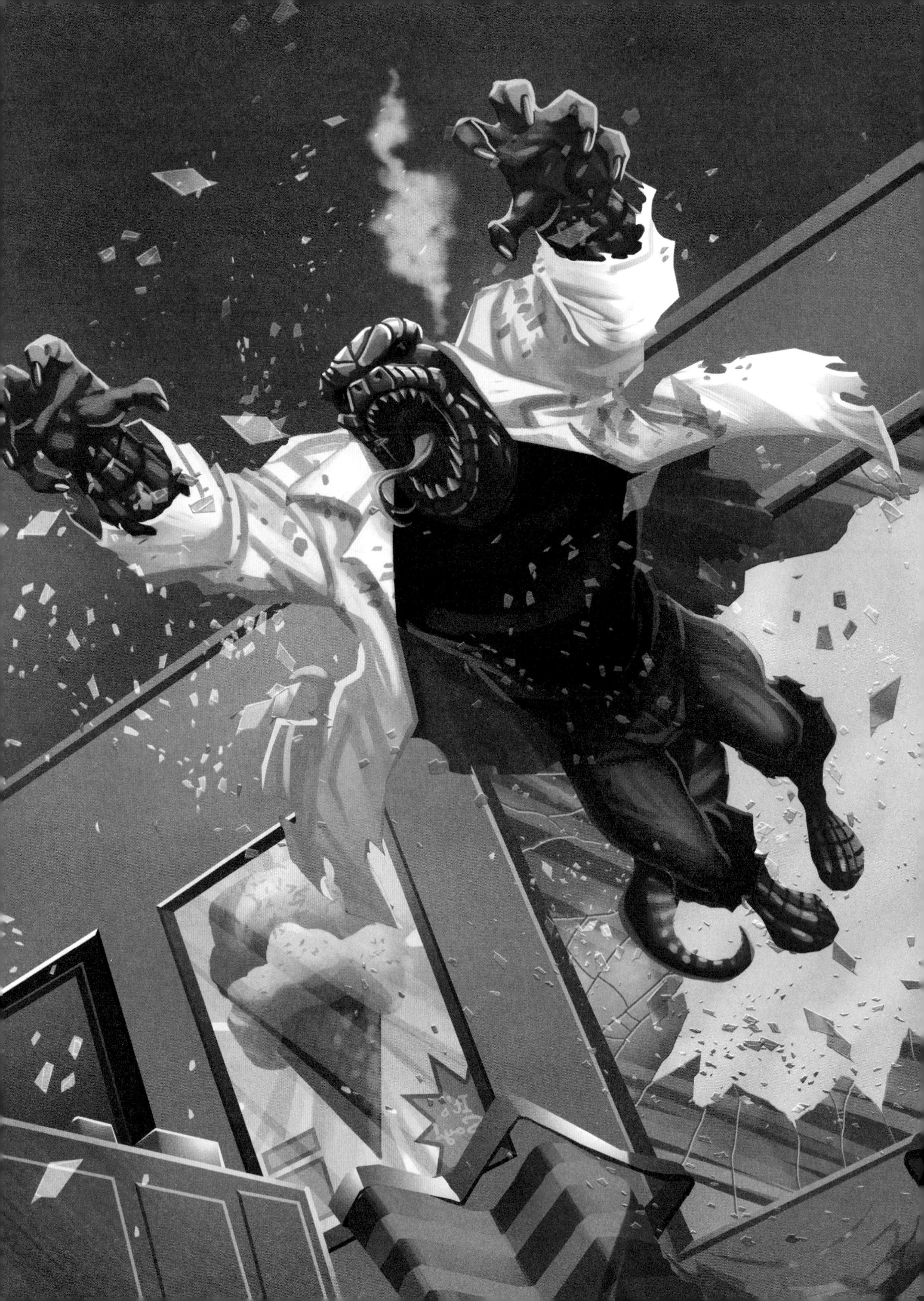

Spidey trailed behind the Lizard as they made their way up the building where Dr. Connors had his lab.

"Once you go in, you're not coming out," Spidey said as he scaled the side of the building.

The Lizard tried to knock Spidey down with his powerful tail, but it didn't work. The Lizard's roar echoed through the streets of the city.

People crowded around to see the excitement atop the building. Spidey was going to save the day!

Spider-Man made his way into the lab, grabbing the antidote. The Lizard crashed through the door, followed by a group of angry reptiles. Spidey knew the Lizard must have given them something to make them so vicious. Suddenly, a snake slithered through the door, making its way toward Spidey.

"Yikes," Spider-Man called out as a small lizard bit his foot and a snake coiled itself around his leg.

Spidey quickly fired webs at the Lizard as more reptiles attacked.

The Lizard fought off the webs, pushing Spider-Man back and swinging his tail at Spidey.

The team of reptiles attacked again, and Spider-Man didn't know if he was going to be able to fight both the Lizard and the many cold-blooded fiends that surrounded him.

Spider-Man was in full battle when the Lizard threw a desk at him. Spidey fell down in pain; his body ached and he didn't know if he would be able to get up.

"Ouch!" Spidey called out, "Dr. Connors, do you realize what you are doing? You have to stop the Lizard!"

But it was pointless. Dr. Connors had no control once the Lizard was unleashed. You couldn't reason with him; you just needed to give him the antidote.

Spidey eyed the antidote as the Lizard seized the opportunity to attack Spider-Man. He ordered the reptiles to hold Spidey down as the Lizard threw a bunch of powerful blows.

Spider-Man tried hard to fight back, but was careful that they didn't bump into the antidote. He didn't want to spill it. Finally Spidey broke free, grabbed the antidote, and poured it onto the Lizard's rough tongue.

Within seconds, the Lizard began to disappear and Dr. Connors reappeared. Spider-Man was very happy to see his friendly and familiar face. The beasts had been tamed, and Mrs. Connors would be happy to see her husband back home.

"Wow, what happened?" Dr. Connors asked.

"It's a long story." Spidey sighed.

Soon, Mrs. Connors had her husband back and J. Jonah
Jameson had his front page spread.

Everyone was happy!

Peter came home to one of Aunt May's amazing home cooked meals.

"How was your day, Peter?" Aunt May asked.

Peter didn't even know where to begin. Aunt May didn't know Peter was Spider-Man, and he certainly couldn't tell her about his fight with the Lizard. "Don't forget to save room for dessert, Peter," Aunt May said as Peter finished his soup. "I picked up a pint of ice cream. Your favorite, Rocky Road."

SPIDER-MAN

The Spectacular Spider-Fan

It was October 31st, and, as he did every Halloween, Peter Parker returned home to help Aunt May hand out candy to neighborhood trick-or-treaters. As group after group of ghosts and witches, astronauts and Super Heroes, came and went, Aunt May couldn't help but remember simpler times.

"Peter, I remember how excited you would get when you were little," she said. "You always loved running around in costumes."

I *still* do, Peter thought, hiding a secret smile.

But then, just as Aunt May dropped another heaping handful of candy into children's bags, Peter's spider-sense started tingling. Danger was near!

Meanwhile, just up the block, little David Dangle and his pals were ringing doorbells and raking in the goods—chocolate, licorice, you name it, they had collected it.

David, as it happened, was dressed as his most favorite of heroes—he had been waiting all year to dress up as the spectacular Spider-Man!

Unfortunately, little David Dangle's timing was terrible....

Other kids started shouting in the distance. David and his friends spun around, alarmed. The villainous Hobgoblin was flying through the night, stealing bags of candy, left and right!

"You aren't *really* Spider-Man, are you?" Hobgoblin shrieked, whirling down toward David. "You're short, you're scrawny, and you're *certainly* no hero."

"I am tonight!" David replied. He knew he was no match for the villain, but had to do whatever he could to keep his neighborhood safe.

"Run, you guys! I've got this!" David shouted, standing his ground as Hobgoblin menaced closer.

Hobgoblin stopped dead in his tracks, hovering right in front of the tiny hero.

"Robbing banks makes me ever so hungry," the villain snarled.

Then, with one swift swipe, Hobgoblin ripped David's bag of candy right from the boy's back!

"I won't let you get away with this!" David said as he targeted the villain with his toy web-shooters.

David sprayed and sprayed and sprayed. He covered the Hobgoblin's face with fake webs!

But the Hobgoblin easily shrugged off the foam, a sneer curling his lips.

"You know, you're just as foolish as the *real* Spider-Man," Hobgoblin chuckled.

"I'll take that as a compliment!" a strong voice called from above.

It was Spider-Man—the *real*, one, true, fantastic, sensational, amazing Spider-Man!

Spidey swung past, grabbing David and carrying him to safety, far from the villain's reach.

"There's nothing foolish about being brave, friendly neighborhood Spider-Fan," Peter began, "but take it from a genuine web-head—this kind of trouble needs to be handled by grown-ups!"

"You got it, Spidey!" David said. He knew the hero was right.

Peter made David promise to stay safe, then lunged back out into the night sky. Spidey shot a web line, diving straight for Hobgoblin.

"Don't think I haven't prepared for this," Hobgoblin
challenged. He reached into his bag and hurled a handful of
razor-sharp, bat-shaped ninja stars right at the wall-crawler.

Spidey twirled around the blades with ease. . .but his web
line didn't. The bat-blades snapped his web, and sent the hero
hurtling toward the hard concrete below!

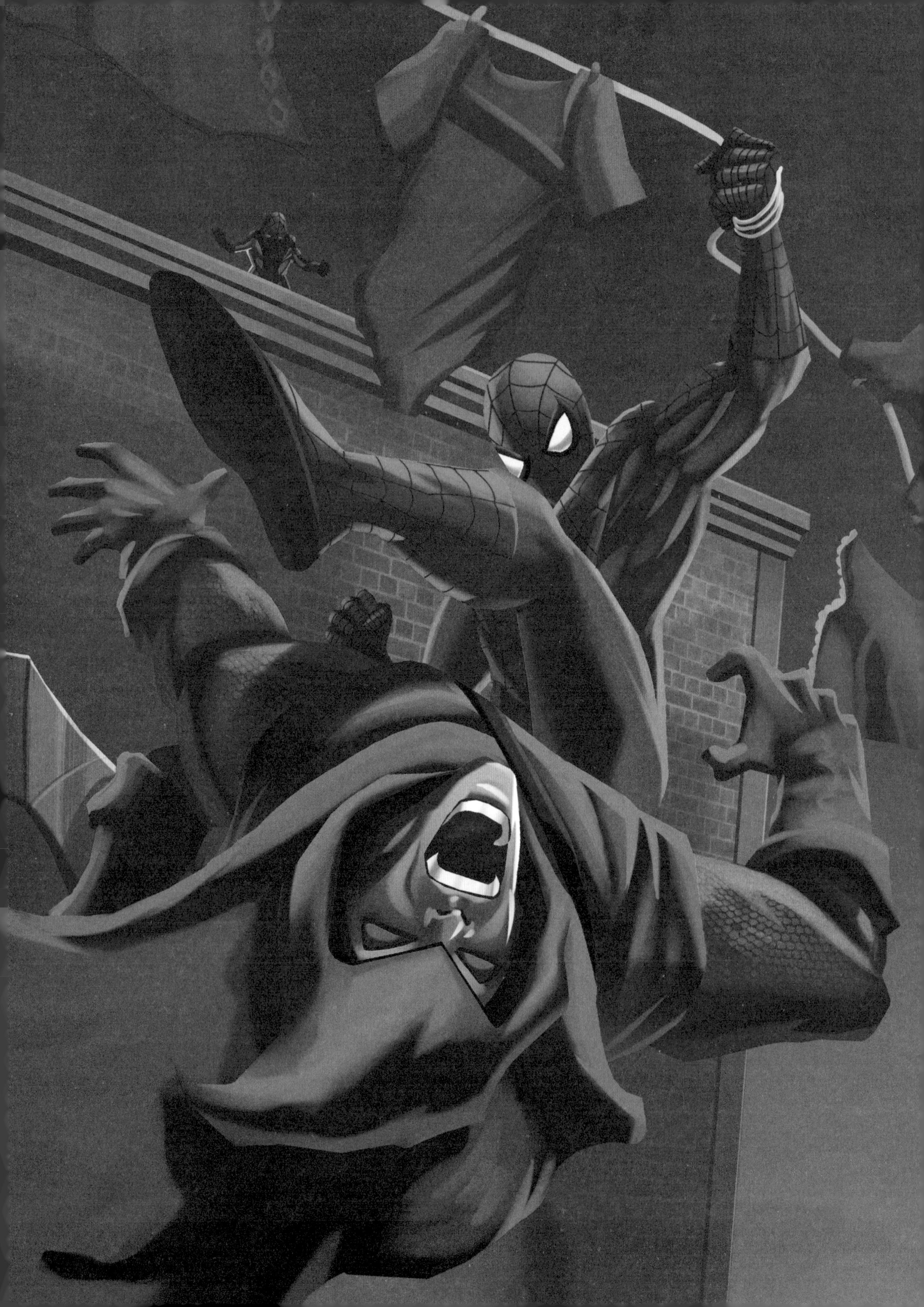

"Grab the clothesline, Spider-Man!" David shouted from above.

"Great idea, Spider-Fan!" Peter called back. Spidey took hold of the clothesline as he fell. Shirts, sweaters, undies, and dresses flew left and right as he swung down into the villain. Spider-Man knocked Hobgoblin from his glider with a mighty kick!

It wasn't long before the police arrived to deal with the defeated villain. Spider-Man made sure to return all of the candy bags to their rightful owners.

"Happy Halloween, kids!" Spidey said as he swung off into the night.

Exhausted and exhilarated, David soon returned home from
his night of adventure. He tackled his mom with a giant bear hug.
"How was your night?" she asked.
David couldn't hide his smile, grinning from ear to ear.

"Mom," he said, "my night was *amazing*!"

Next year, Peter thought, maybe I'll go trick-or-treating as my new hero.

And just who was that new hero?

It was a little Spider-Fan named David Dangle!

MARVEL SPIDER-MAN

Mysterio Attacks!

Thwip! Spider-Man shot a web across Fifth Avenue and swung past the Empire State Building on his way toward *The Daily Bugle.* Peter Parker was late for work, and the only thing that could get him there in time was his web-shooters.

"Great," Peter said to himself as he fired another web line. "If I'm late for work again, Mr. Jameson is going to explode!"

Just then, an explosion of green and purple smoke erupted from the top floor of *The Daily Bugle* building!

"Yikes! I didn't think he'd *literally* explode!" Spidey said as saw the blast. "Better get in there to see if anyone needs help."

Landing on the side of the building, Spider-Man crawled up the wall, through a window, and into the smoky office—but the office was empty!

That's when Spidey heard a booming voice coming from the newsroom and his spider-sense started to tingle.

"Now that I have your attention," the bizarre voice began, "you will all be witness to the total destruction of *The Daily Bugle!*"

Spider-Man recognized that voice—it was his enemy Mysterio, the master of illusion!

Spidey crept to the door and opened it a crack so he could see what was going on. The menacing Mysterio was holding J. Jonah Jameson by the collar and was addressing the staff.

"No one can help you, Jameson, not even Spider-Man!" the villain hissed.

"That's my cue!" Spidey said as he lunged through the door and launched himself at the villain.

Spider-Man caught Mysterio by surprise and the two tumbled to the ground, locked in combat! As the Super Hero and Super Villain continued to fight, Jameson crawled to the exit but was surprised to see that all the doors had been locked from the outside.

They were trapped!

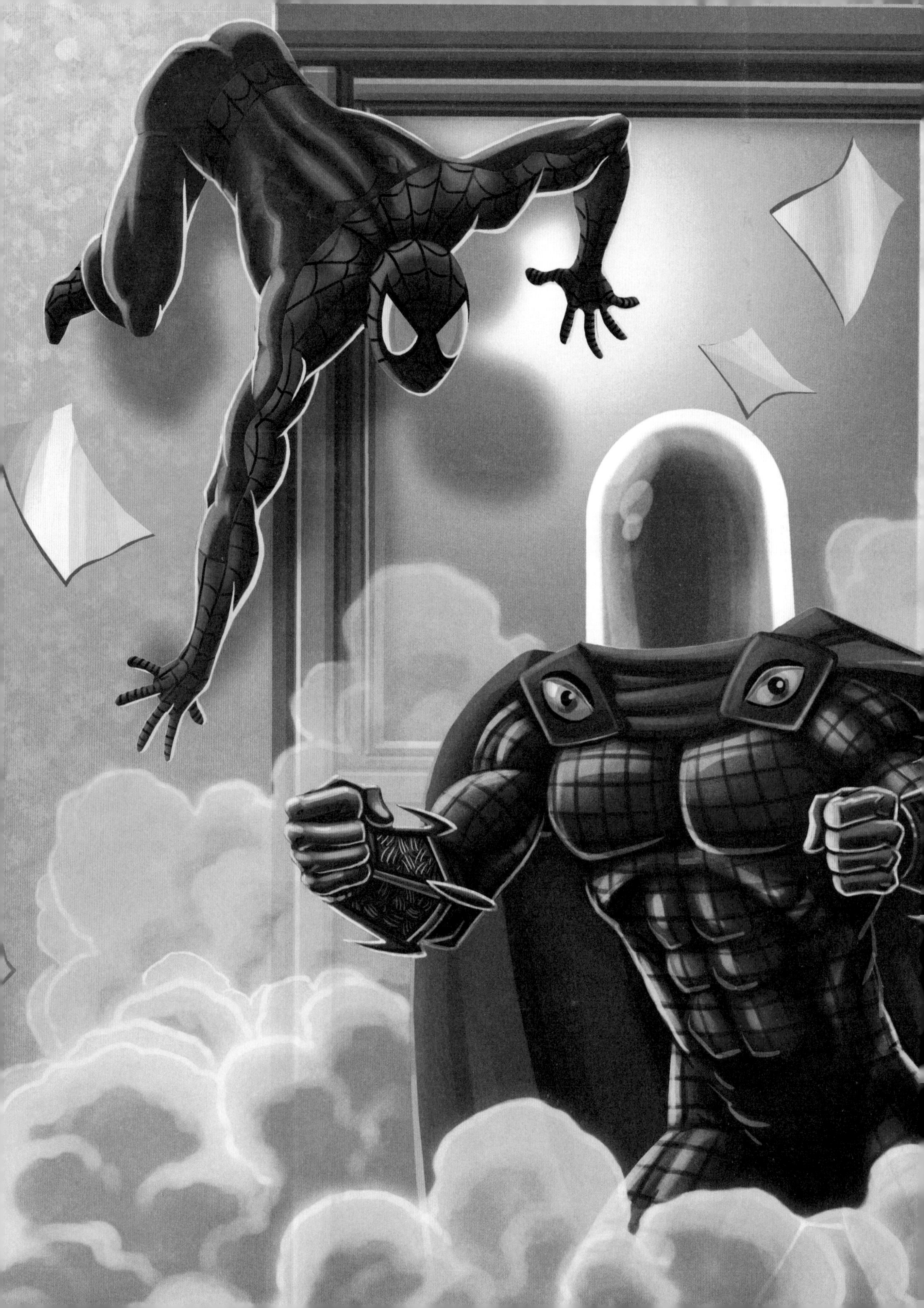

"The amazing Spider-Man!" Mysterio began. "Right on time...
to meet your doom!"

Mysterio raised his arms and the newsroom filled with thick
green smoke. Then the villain disappeared into the fog right
before everyone's eyes!

"Meet *my* doom?" Spider-Man said. "What do you suppose
he meant by *that*?"

Mysterio's voice suddenly echoed across the room. "When I first appeared, J. Jonah Jameson promised that he could deliver Spider-Man," the villain said. "Instead, I was defeated by Spider-Man . . . and now, you will *all* pay—starting with Jameson!"

Spidey knew he had to act fast! Just as Mysterio appeared from the smoke, Spider-Man fired a web line and swung toward the villain.

With unbelievable strength and speed, the amazing Spider-Man kicked Mysterio in the chest and then fired another web line at Jameson, sticking him to the wall.

"Sorry to disappoint you, Mysterio, but I don't have plans to meet my doom for at least another sixty or seventy years!" Spidey said.

Spider-Man stood above the trapped Mysterio and removed the villain's domed helmet. But Spidey was shocked at the person he saw beneath the mask: it was Peter Parker!

"Parker!" Jameson yelled. "*You're* Mysterio?!?"

Mysterio was a master of disguise, but only Spider-Man knew that the villain wasn't *really* Peter Parker. This must've been the disguise he was going to use in order to escape, Spidey thought. But how was Spider-Man going to save everyone in *The Daily Bugle* and prove that Mysterio wasn't Peter?

While all these thoughts ran through Spidey's mind, the villain leaped forward and attacked!

Ow, I hit hard! Spidey thought to himself as he picked himself up off the floor. As Mysterio delivered another blow, Spider-Man rolled across the smoky room.

Spidey looked around the office, and realized that everyone was at work—all but one person. The only person who wasn't there was the person who was late—Peter Parker. *That's* why Mysterio used him for his disguise, Spidey thought. And that gave the wall-crawler an idea!

Spidey jumped across the room and crawled along the wall, completely hidden by the smoke. He grabbed a hoodie off a desk, wrapped it around himself, and removed his mask.

Just then, the real Peter Parker appeared through the smoke. "Hey, guys. Sorry I'm late!"

Mysterio turned, shocked. "No! How did *you* get in?" the villain shouted.

"*Two* Parkers?" Jameson said, confused. "Next there will be two Spider-Men!"

"Not if *I* have anything to say about it!" Mysterio yelled.

The appearance of the real Peter Parker had worked. While everyone was distracted, Peter ducked beneath the smoke, put his mask back on, and charged at Mysterio.

Firing both web-shooters again and again, the amazing Spider-Man captured Mysterio in a giant spiderweb for all to see.

Then with a *CRASH!*, the police finally broke into the newsroom, just as Spider-Man jumped out the nearest window. "Here you go, boys," Spidey said to the cops as he swung away. "One gift-wrapped Super Villain, courtesy of you-know-who!"

A few minutes later, the real Peter Parker entered the newsroom. J. Jonan Jameson, who was still stuck to the side of the wall, looked down at his star photographer. "Parker," JJJ said, "You're late!"

Peter sighed. It was just another day at the office for Peter Parker. . .and your friendly neighborhood Spider-Man!

Nova's on the Job

Peter Parker didn't usually have time to hang around—but here he was, hanging from the top of a skyscraper with nothing to do. No Super Villains to fight, no citizens to save, no sirens to follow. It had been like this for a whole week.

The amazing Spider-Man. . .bored.

I bet Iron Man never runs out of things to do, Spider-Man thought, staring at his reflection.

He started doodling on the side of the building to keep himself occupied.

Suddenly, Spider-Man's spider-sense began to tingle. "Finally," Spidey said, "some action!" With a practiced ease, Spider-Man leaped down toward the street and caught his reflection in a store window.

"Maybe it's Sandman," Peter said, imagining to himself. "I could use a day at the beach."

Spider-Man followed the sirens all the way to City Hall. There, he found a team of police officers looking up at the building's roof.

"Did someone call for a little amazing?" Spider-Man asked.

"Spider-Man! Thank goodness you're here! Sandman—he's kidnapped the mayor!" Just then, Sandman appeared on the top of the building!

Yes! It *is* Sandman! Spidey thought. Am I good, or am I good?

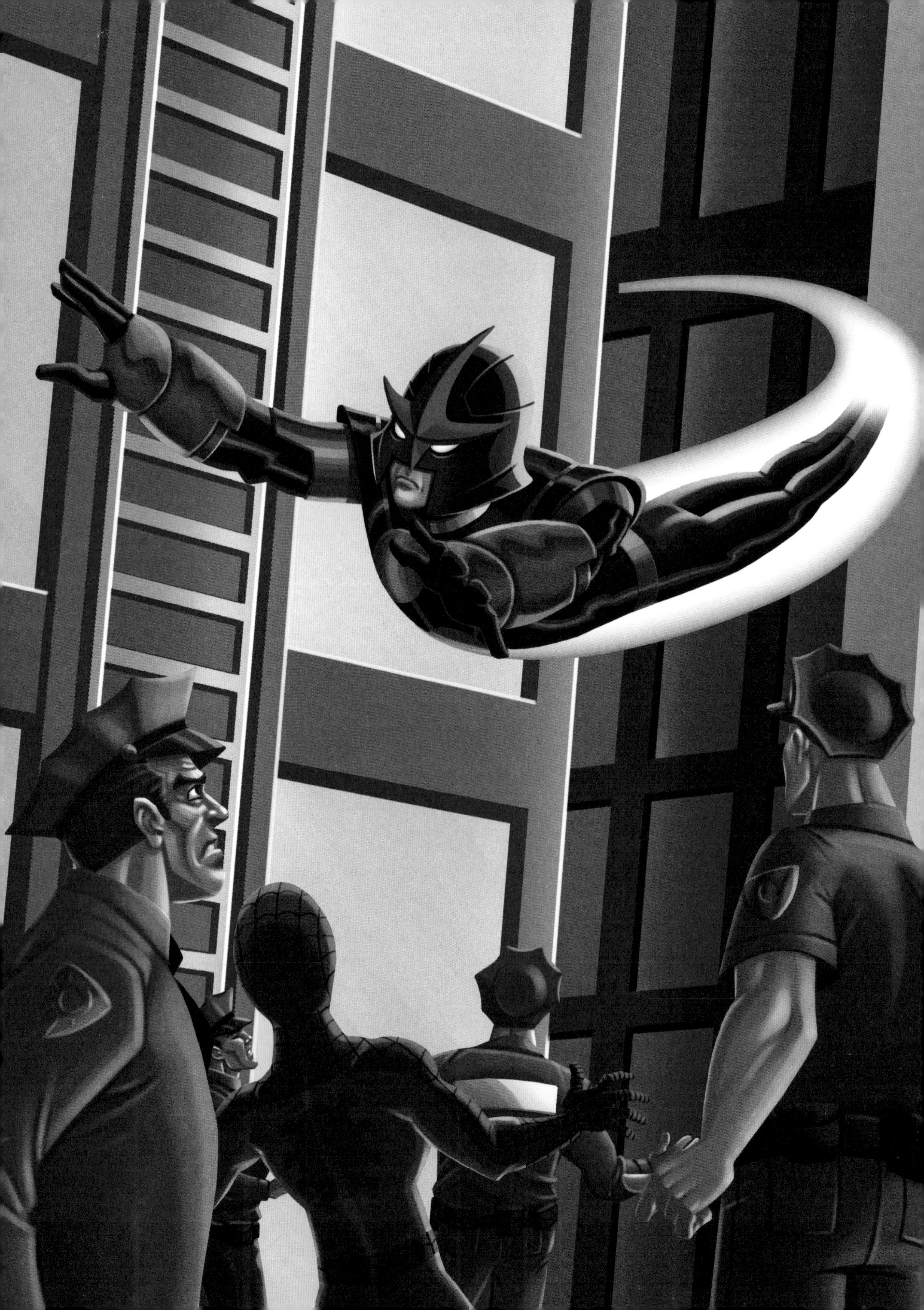

"Don't worry! I'll be back with the mayor before you can say—" But before Spider-Man could say anything, a bolt of blue light flashed through the sky.

"It's a bird!"

"It's a plane!"

"No, it's Nova," Spider-Man said, disappointed.

"Nova?" the police officer asked Spider-Man.

"A Super Hero with crazy space powers. He can fly, lift super heavy things, and steal the spotlight in less than three seconds flat."

Spider-Man knew that being a Super Hero was more than getting attention. It was a privilege—and a responsibility.

But there was something about Nova that drove Spider-Man crazy.

Spider-Man quickly realized that the police officer was much more interested in the exciting fight between Sandman and Nova than his sob story.

"Get ready to taste my fist, Nova!" Sandman roared.

"I doubt it! Fighting you is like a day at the beach!" Nova replied.

"Man—he even stole my joke!" Spider-Man said under his breath.

With a supersonic punch, Nova knocked Sandman out.
The police officers cheered.

"I don't know what we would have done without you, Nova,"
the mayor said.

Fortunately, Spidey didn't have to listen to Nova's fans for long.
His spidey-sense began to tingle again. Someone needed help!

Spider-Man swung his way across town to a large bank.
Three men in masks were stealing money from the safe.

"Did you guys forget your ATM cards?" Spider-Man said
as he swung in.

"Oh, no, it's the Spider!"
one of the robbers said.

"That's Spider-*Man*," Peter said, as he used
his web-shooter to knock the stolen money
out of the robber's hands.

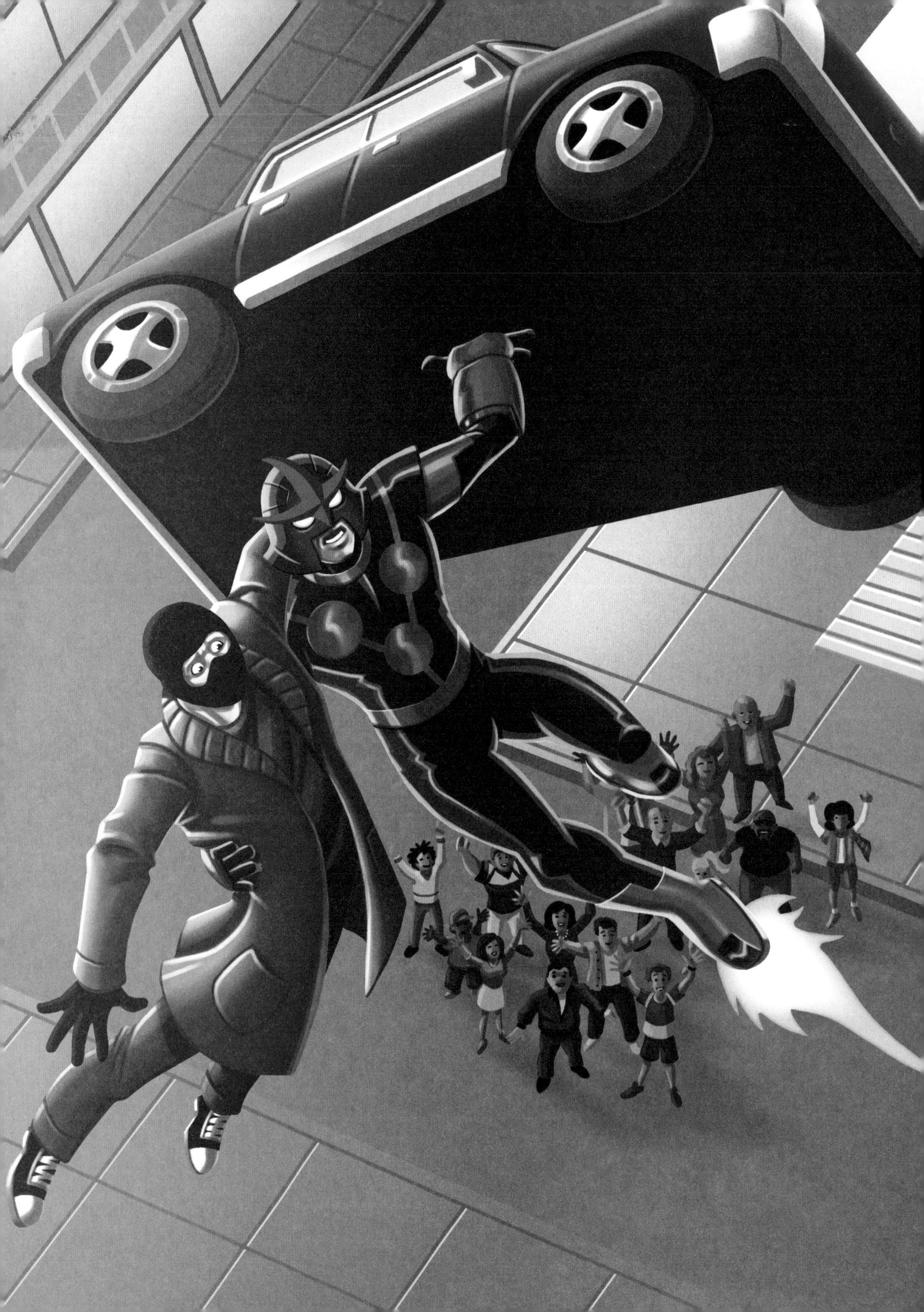

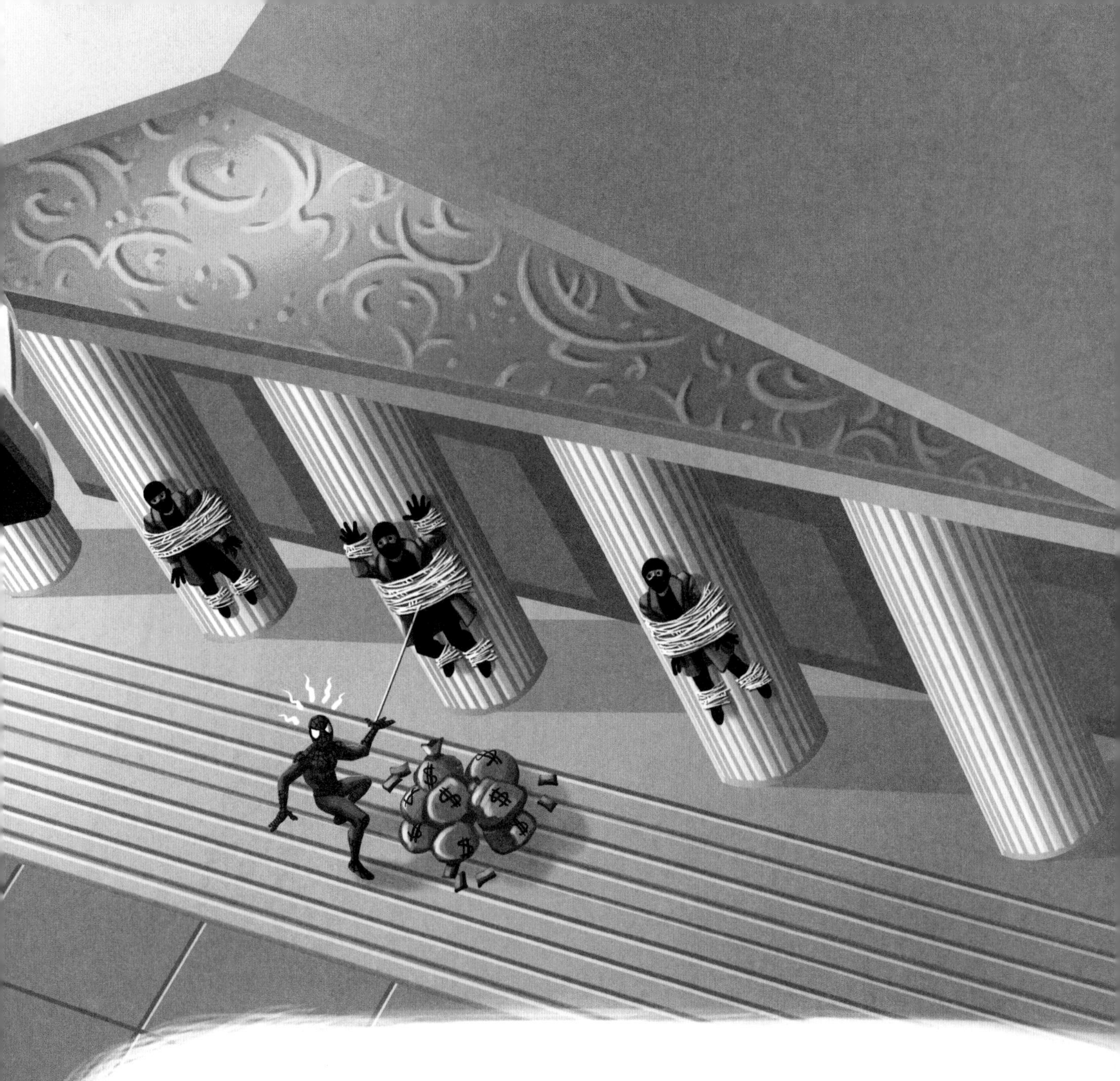

Spider-Man led the three robbers outside. But just then, Nova flew down, carrying a car in one hand and a very worried fourth robber in the other.

Peter had forgotten about the getaway car!

"Looks like you lost something, Spider," Nova said.

"Spider-MAN!" Peter said. But no one heard him. They were all cheering for Nova.

The next day, Peter was back to doing nothing. At least I'm improving my artistic skills, he thought, as he put the finishing touches on a Nova web sculpture.

He was so busy admiring his handiwork, that he almost didn't hear the sirens. Peter looked down and saw police cars racing uptown.

I'll just let Nova deal with that, Spider-Man thought.

But Spider-Man couldn't ignore his spider-sense, and more importantly, he couldn't ignore people in trouble. He quickly jumped off the roof and swung toward the sirens.

Nova was fighting the Lizard on the Brooklyn Bridge.

The Lizard looked tired, but Nova wasn't even breaking a sweat!

Well, I guess I'm not needed here after all, Spider-Man thought.

He turned around, about to head back home, when he felt a tug on his costume. He looked down and saw a little boy.

"Mr. Spider-Man, sir. Can you help me?"

Spider-Man kneeled down. "Sure. What do you need, kid?"

"I can't find Puddles anywhere—he's my dog."

Spider-Man sighed. Dog-catching wasn't exactly as epic as fighting the Lizard on a crowded bridge. But Spider-Man was happy he could help somebody.

"All right, where did you last see him?" he asked.

Before long, Spider-Man found the boy's dog hiding in some bushes near the bridge. "Looks like he didn't like the noise of all that fighting," Spider-Man said, as he gave the dog back to the young boy.

"Thanks, Spider-Man!" the boy said.

"It's what I do!" Spider-Man replied.

The boy glanced back at the fight on the bridge. "Mr. Spider-Man, do you think Nova will be okay?"

"Nova's going to be just fine. He's a hero."

"Just like you?"

"Yes, just like me."

The boy smiled. That smile made Spider-Man feel as good as a thankful mayor or a cheering crowd. Well, almost as good. Cheering crowds *were* pretty hard to beat.

As Spider-Man jumped into the air he felt his spider-sense tingling.

"Here we go again." He smiled to himself. Nova couldn't possibly beat him to the villain this time. . .right?

Spider-Man and the Avengers

"**I**ron Man," Captain America said. "Quick status report: how bad?"

Iron Man looked around. "Well, it's not good, Cap. This is the work of Korvac, a sort of human supercomputer," Iron Man explained. "He can take over any computer system anywhere, easily."

"You're right. That's *not* good," Captain America admitted.

"Korvac can also tap into any energy source and use it to generate devastating blasts," Iron Man said. "And as we can clearly see, he's using both powers to wreak havoc."

"Sounds like a challenge," Captain America said.

The ground shook as the mighty Thor and the incredible Hulk landed with a loud thud. "Has the madman informed us of his goal?" Thor asked.

"Judging by what he's accomplished so far," Iron Man said, "I'd guess total devastation of New York City, at least to start. I know that's usually your department, Hulk."

"Nick Fury at S.H.I.E.L.D. hasn't been able to find out anything," Captain America said. "Black Widow's in the subway and Hawkeye's at the airport—they said things are crazy everywhere."

"Hey, it's the Avengers! Hi!" Spider-Man said as he swung toward the team. "Aw, you started without me."

"Hey, I don't mean to, you know, be *that guy*," Spider-Man said, "but there are some airplanes up there that I think are in trouble."

Without a word, Hulk grabbed Thor and threw him.

Thor whirled his mighty hammer in a circle so quickly that a small cyclone formed.

The airplanes were sucked in. . .and found themselves circling New York safely.

Down below, Spider-Man said, "I could have done that. If I'd thought of it."

"Bug man funny," Hulk said.

"Somehow," Spider-Man replied, "even your compliments sound scary."

"We're a bit busy trying to keep the entire city from perishing, so if you could just run along?" Iron Man said.

"Yeah, you're sure doing a bang-up job so far," Spider-Man replied. "Have you found what's behind all this craziness?"

"It's a villain named Korvac," Captain America replied.

"The living computer guy?" Spider-Man asked.

The craziness continued as Hulk stopped two buses from colliding into each other. Korvac was out of control. "You're familiar with Korvac?" asked Captain America.

"Well, we don't exactly go out for coffee or anything," Spider-Man said. "He was created by an alien race, right? Did you run a trace for their DNA?"

"We...uh..." Iron Man said. "We've been kind of busy— you know, saving people."

"You've never heard of multitasking?" Spider-Man asked
Iron Man.

Iron Man used his armor to run a quick DNA trace. "Nice work,
kid. We've got his location."

"Great. But this guy's nearly unstoppable, right?" Spider-Man
asked. "So how are you going to, you know. . .stop him?"

"Iron Man?" Captain America said. "Any thoughts?"

"Spider-Man here's doing well so far," Iron Man said. "What's your solution, junior?"

"How about we overload him?" Spider-Man suggested.

"I can reroute my repulsor beam to fire a single shot from my chest plate," Iron Man said.

"Then Thor hits him with a bolt of lighting!" Spider-Man added.

"Good plan, son. Avengers—and Spider-Man—Assemble!" Cap yelled as the heroes jumped into action.

The Super Heroes landed on the rubble just below Korvac. "If this doesn't work, I'm going to be powerless," Iron Man said.

"You're also going to be a sitting duck," Spider-Man added.

"Hold on. . ." Iron Man said, concerned that the plan might not work.

"Way to take one for the team, I.M.," Spider-Man said. "We're proud of you."

"All right, Avengers," Cap said. "It's time to take down Korvac!"

But Korvac sensed them coming. The moment they landed, he attacked.

"Now!" Iron Man yelled.

Spidey and the Avengers tried to shield Korvac's blast while fighting him off. Korvac fired a beam at Cap, who deflected it with his vibranium shield.

The blast bounced back and hit Hulk, knocking him off the rooftop! Spidey was fast and dodged the next blast as he spun a web at Korvac. With the villain distracted by the web-slinger, Iron Man powered up and prepared to fire just as Thor called down the lightning.

Thor unleashed a massive lightning bolt, striking Korvac.
At the same time, Iron Man redirected all of his repulsor
energy through his chest piece and fired a blast at Korvac.
Meanwhile, Spidey shot webs at
Korvac in attempt to distract him.
Their grand plan was in action!
It worked.

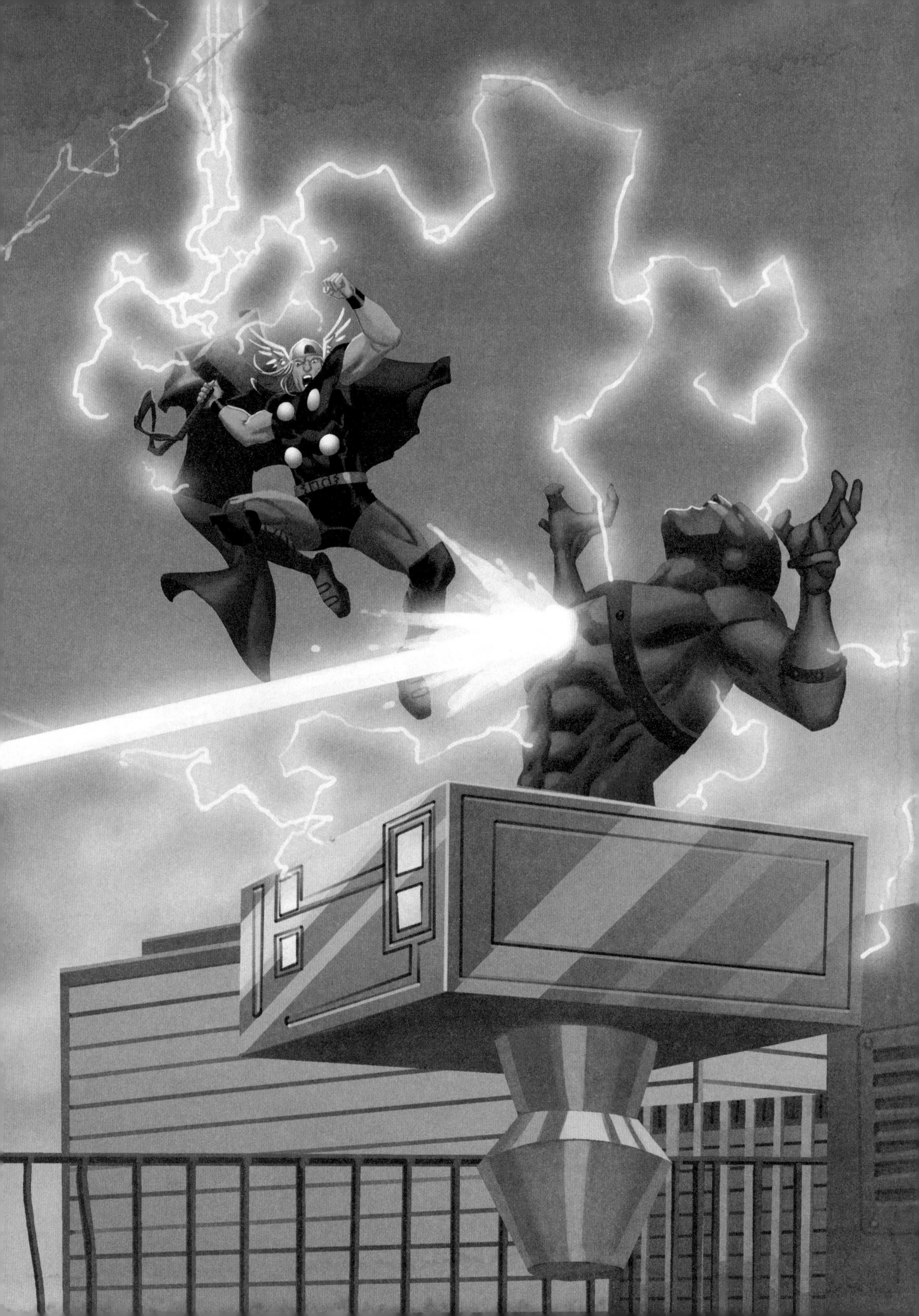

Korvac collapsed and so did his grip on the city's computer and power systems.

"I don't get paid nearly enough for this job," Iron Man said with an exhausted sigh.

Spider-Man started to laugh, then stopped. "Wait. . .you guys don't *really* get paid for this, do you?"

"This isn't about money, it's about helping people. There's no better reward!" Captain America said.

"I was kidding!" Spider-Man said. "I'm just happy to have teamed up with the mighty Avengers!"

The End